Holly could see Anne Fairfax standing at the centre of attention, holding something high in her hands. Something that flashed in the sunlight.

Holly came to a skidding halt, her mouth falling open.

'What?' panted Belinda. 'What is it?'

'It's a gold statue,' breathed Holly.

'Wow!' gasped Tracy. 'They've really found something!'

'But don't you see?' whispered Holly. 'It's exactly the same as the one we saw in the museum guide. And *exactly* the same as the one that fell out of the rucksack.'

'Are you sure?' said Belinda. 'It can't be.'

'It is,' said Holly. 'And you know what that means, don't you? It means this whole thing is a *fake*!'

The Mystery Club series

Buried Secrets
The Mystery Club 8

Fiona Kelly

Hodder
Children's
Books

a division of Hodder Headline plc

Special thanks to Allan Frewin Jones

Copyright © by Ben M. Baglio 1994
Created by Ben M. Baglio
London W6 0HE
First published in Great Britain in 1994 by Knight Books

10 9 8 7 6 5 4 3 2

A Catalogue record for this book is
available from the British Library

ISBN 0 340 60724 6

Typeset by Hewer Text Composition Services, Edinburgh
Printed and bound in Great Britain by
Cox & Wyman Ltd, Reading, Berkshire

Hodder Children's Books
A Division of Hodder Headline plc
338 Euston Road
London NW1 3BH

1 Digging up a story

'What is it? What's happened?' Tracy Foster came bursting into the classroom where her Mystery Club friends, Holly Adams and Belinda Hayes, were sitting. 'Jamie said you needed me urgently. I came right away.'

Holly smiled at her. 'It wasn't *that* urgent,' she said. Tracy was dressed in tennis kit, her blonde hair caught back in a white sweatband. It looked like she'd run all the way from the school tennis courts.

Belinda laughed, looking at Holly through her wire-framed spectacles. 'I told you it would work,' she said.

It had been Belinda's idea to send Holly's younger brother, Jamie, out in search of Tracy.

'What would work?' Tracy said suspiciously, walking over to the desk where her two friends were sitting. 'This had better be good,' she said. 'I was winning two sets to love out there.'

Holly, tall and slim with short brown hair, held a pen poised over the Mystery Club's red notebook. Opposite her Belinda lounged across two chairs

1

with her feet up, a half-eaten chocolate bar in one fist, looking her usual lazy and dishevelled self.

Holly smiled up at Tracy's anxious, excited face. 'I need some help,' she said. 'I can't think of anything to write for the next issue of the school magazine, and Steffie wants something by early next week.'

'*What*?' yelled Tracy. 'You can't be serious! I was thrashing Jenny Fairbright two sets to love, and four games to love in the final set, and you drag me all the way over here for *that*? To help you write an *article*?' Tracy's American accent deepened. Three years of living in the small Yorkshire town of Willow Dale had softened it, but it always came back when she was angry or excited.

'I should have brought my racket with me,' she said. 'I could have beaten you both to death with it. I thought you were in some kind of trouble.'

'I am,' said Holly. 'If I miss Steffie's deadline I'm going to look really stupid, especially as I promised her something special this time.'

If Holly had a rival at the Winifred Bowen-Davies School, it was Steffie Smith, the editor of *Winformation*, the school magazine. Holly and her family had only been in Willow Dale a few months. They had moved up from London when Holly's mother had been promoted, and Holly's first attempts at getting herself involved in the life of her new school had been to approach Steffie Smith to write for the magazine.

Holly had put a piece in the magazine, advertising for people to join the Mystery Club that she hoped to set up. A club for people who liked reading mystery novels. Steffie had cut the advert down to a single, uninspiring sentence.

Despite this, Tracy and Belinda had arrived for the first Mystery Club meeting and the three girls had been firm friends ever since.

Although, by the expression on Tracy's face at that moment, it looked as if their friendship was coming under some strain.

'But I was *winning*!' exclaimed Tracy. 'I was beating Jenny Fairbright, you idiots. The school champion.'

'It's only a game,' said Belinda with a yawn. 'It's not like it was anything important. Anyway,' she said with a grin, 'too much exercise is bad for you – I read it somewhere. Superfit people are collapsing with heart attacks all over the place.'

'Then you've got nothing to worry about,' said Tracy. 'If being a lazy, idle lump is good for you, you should live to be a hundred.'

'Do you two think you could put the personal abuse on hold for a while?' said Holly. She looked up at Tracy. 'I'm sorry about messing up your game, but this *is* important. You know what Steffie's like. She'd just love to get one over on

3

me. I've really got to think of something brilliant for the magazine.'

'Did I hear the word brilliant?' called a voice from the doorway. 'Are you talking about me?'

'I can't say the word "brilliant" and the name "Kurt Welford" have even been linked in my mind,' said Belinda, as Kurt came into the room.

Kurt grinned. He was used to Belinda's sense of humour, and her opinion of boys in general. Tall and blond, his main link with the Mystery Club was as Tracy's part-time boyfriend.

He smiled at Tracy. 'I thought you were spending your lunch-break playing tennis?' he said. 'What happened?'

'This pair happened,' said Tracy. 'Would you believe they dragged me all the way over here to help them come up with an article for the school magazine?'

'What sort of article do you want?' asked Kurt.

'If I knew that I wouldn't be sitting here with a blank page in front of me,' Holly said impatiently. 'What I'd really like to do is to get an interview with P J Benson. Now that would be my idea of a brilliant article.' P J Benson was Holly's favourite writer. She had written many of the mystery books that filled Holly's shelves at home. Holly sighed. 'But I don't suppose I'll ever manage something as grand as that.'

'What about something on cricket?' suggested Kurt. 'I could help write it.'

4

Belinda yawned again. 'Fascinating,' she said. 'People could read it last thing at night as a cure for insomnia.'

'I suppose you'd prefer something on horses?' said Kurt.

'That's a thought,' Belinda said brightly. 'We could do an interview with Meltdown.' Meltdown was Belinda's horse, a gift from her wealthy parents.

'No it isn't,' Holly said firmly. 'For heaven's sake, you lot, isn't *anything* interesting going on around here?'

'There's that dig over at Hob's Mound,' said Kurt. 'That sounds like it might be interesting.' He gave Belinda a cool smile. 'But I don't suppose you'll want to hear about that.'

'What dig?' asked Holly. 'Digging for what?'

'Buried treasure,' said Kurt. 'So I've heard, anyway.'

'Ignore him,' said Belinda. 'He's winding us up.'

'Am I?' said Kurt. 'I needn't bother telling you all about it, then, if it's not really happening.'

'Take no notice of Belinda,' said Holly. 'Come on, Kurt, let us in on it. What's going on?'

'The university has set up an archaeological dig at Hob's Mound,' explained Kurt. 'Do you know the place?'

'I do,' said Tracy. 'It's out west of here, isn't it?'

'That's right,' said Belinda. 'It's just a big grassy

5

lump in the middle of a field. I go riding with Meltdown over that way sometimes. Isn't there some story about it being haunted or something?'

Kurt nodded. 'That's the place. You can tell it's not a natural part of the countryside by the shape of it.' He described a smooth dome in the air with his hand. 'Sitting there in the middle of all these flat fields. They've known for ages that it was a Celtic burial mound. It was investigated seventy or eighty years ago, but nothing was found. Apparently they just went at it with a shovel in those days, so it was easy to miss things. But now they've got computer-enhanced photography to help them. They've got hold of some new evidence that suggests someone pretty important might be buried in there. Some Celtic chieftain or other. So the university has funded a new excavation.' Kurt smiled round at the three girls. 'And they started digging this morning.'

Holly wrote 'Hob's Mound' in her notebook. 'Hold on, though,' she said. 'How come you know all about this? It hasn't been in the papers.'

Kurt grinned. 'Not yet it hasn't,' he said. 'But don't forget, my dad is editor of the *Express*. He gets all this sort of information before everyone else. And he's asked me to go over there this afternoon to take some photos.'

The *Express* was Willow Dale's local newspaper, and Kurt had often been sent off with his camera to cover special events.

'We could have a real scoop here,' said Holly. 'Think of the headlines: "Schoolgirls help to find ancient buried treasure".'

'Ancient, mouldy, horrible old bones, you mean,' said Tracy. 'Where's the treasure come into it?'

'Don't you know *anything*?' said Belinda. 'In ancient times when they buried someone important they always surrounded them with gold and jewels and stuff like that. Haven't you ever heard of Tutankhamen, and all the amazing stuff they found in the place where he was buried?' She looked at Kurt. 'That's right, isn't it?'

Kurt nodded. 'It's not likely to be anything as fantastic as they found in Egypt, but there could certainly be some interesting things in there.'

Tracy shook her head. 'I never did get the hang of why they did that. What's the use of all that stuff to someone who's dead?'

'It was for them to use in the after-life,' said Holly. 'They believed that the spirit of the dead person would be able to take all their possessions off to the next world with them.'

Tracy gave Kurt a thoughtful look. 'And they reckon all this stuff is still going to be in there, after all this time?'

'That's the idea,' said Kurt. 'With any luck I'm going to get a photo of them finding something amazing. I hope so, anyway. I'm going straight over there from school this afternoon.'

Holly grinned at her friends. 'In that case,' she

7

said, 'I think we ought to go with you. Steffie Smith will be *green* if we come back with the scoop of the century.'

'Is that settled, then?' said Tracy. 'Can I get back to beating the living daylights out of Jenny Fairbright now, or is there something *else* you desperately need me for?'

'You could nip up to the canteen and get me a couple of sandwiches,' said Belinda, staring down at the empty chocolate wrapper. 'I'm starving.'

'Dream on,' said Tracy. 'Get your own sand-wiches – you could do with the exercise. Coming over to the tennis courts with me, Kurt?'

'We'll meet outside after school,' called Holly as Tracy and Kurt headed for the door. 'Don't be late.'

'Well?' said Belinda to Holly after the others had gone. 'Are you happy now you've got something lined up for the magazine? Can we get back to something a bit more important now?'

'Like what?' asked Holly.

'Like getting over to the ice-cream parlour before the end of break,' said Belinda, heaving herself up.

The two girls headed for the school gates, Holly's mind already working on an opening sentence for her article.

'Important archaeological finds discovered near Willow Dale. Your reporter, Holly Adams, was at Hob's Mound as the ancient site was opened up for the first time in over a thousand years.'

8

Yes, she thought. *That* would shut Steffie Smith up once and for all. Especially if Kurt was right, and the mound turned out to be full of priceless antiquities.

She could hardly wait.

It was a fine, breezy afternoon as the four friends cycled through the outskirts of Willow Dale and began the long, slow climb into the countryside.

Holly couldn't resist a glance over her shoulder at the small town that she had grown to love. Beyond the modern buildings, the shopping mall and the ice-rink and the multiplex cinema complex, she could see the church spire and the roofs of the old centre of Willow Dale, lying peacefully under a cheerful sky. Clouds sailed like galleons over the hills.

On days such as this, the noise and bustle of London, where Holly had grown up, seemed a whole world away. She was still in regular contact with her old friends Miranda Hunt and Peter Hamilton, and in her frequent letters to them she had explained that the apparent serenity of Willow Dale was deceptive. Since the Mystery Club had been formed, Holly and her friends had found themselves entangled in some extraordinary real-life adventures. The three girls seemed to attract danger and intrigue like a magnet.

After about a mile, the road levelled out and the four cyclists snaked their way out into the fields.

9

It was only a little way further on that Kurt brought his bicycle to a halt at the grass verge. He pointed across the road.

'There you are,' he said. 'Hob's Mound.'

Beyond a low barrier of bushes, punctuated by a wide wooden gate, Holly saw a stretch of grassy fields. A couple of hundred metres away a long, low hill lifted itself like a huge, upturned bath. Kurt had been right; it certainly didn't look like a natural part of the landscape.

A battered old brown car was parked half off the road near the gate.

The gate was open, and as they pushed their bikes through into the field, Holly saw two Land-rovers parked to one side, and behind them, the square grey shape of a caravan.

A wide strip of turf had been sheared away from the side of the hill and three or four young people were busy with spades and trowels.

But they hardly had time to take this in before the sound of raised voices drew their attention.

The door of the small caravan was open. A woman stood on the steps. An elderly man was shouting and waving a walking-stick towards the mound. The woman seemed to be in her late twenties, dressed in jeans and a loose shirt, her black hair pulled back off her face and tied into a pony-tail. The man wore a shabby brown suit, his grey hair a wild, unkempt thatch over his collar.

10

'Looks like trouble,' said Belinda. 'You don't often see *him* out and about.'

'Who is he?' asked Tracy. 'The landowner?'

Belinda shook her head. 'That's Professor Rothwell,' she said. 'He lives in the Black Mill. You must know it. Over by the River Skelter.' She looked round at her friends. 'Haven't you heard of the Mad Professor? He lives all alone in this big old water mill. He's a total recluse. Never comes out.'

'Well,' said Tracy, 'he looks real mad right now. And he's going to damage someone with that stick if he keeps waving it around like that.'

'Professor Rothwell?' said Kurt. 'I've heard of him, but I've never seen him before. He's a retired don from the university, isn't he? What do you think's brought him over here?'

'There's one way to find out,' said Holly, pushing her bike on through the tall grass. 'Let's go and see.'

'Watch out for that stick,' warned Belinda. 'According to my mother, he's a complete fruitcake.' Belinda's mother was a leading light of Willow Dale society. She knew absolutely everything about everyone in the town.

'How come you know him?' asked Tracy, as they followed Holly's lead towards the caravan.

'I come riding over this way on Meltdown,' explained Belinda. 'Professor Rothwell lives only a kilometre or so further down the road. I've seen him pottering about in the woods. I don't get too

11

close, though. He's given me some extremely peculiar looks in the past.'

'You are committing sacrilege,' they heard the old man shout. 'This place should be left in peace.'

The woman's voice was placatory, but had a hard edge to it. As if she were someone who was not used to being argued with.

'Professor Rothwell, I've got written permission from the university and from the local council,' she said. 'This is a perfectly legitimate archaeological excavation. I don't have time to stand here arguing with you. If you've got any complaints, then make them through the appropriate channels.'

The hefty walking-stick whipped through the air, making the woman step back into the doorway of the caravan.

'I'm warning you, Fairfax,' shouted the old man. 'If you carry on with this desecration, you and everyone here will suffer for it.'

The woman's eyes blazed. 'Are you threatening me?'

'I'm *warning* you,' said Professor Rothwell. 'For your own good. You're interfering with ancient powers.'

The woman ran a hand over her forehead. 'I've been patient with you, Professor,' she said. '*More* than patient. I'm a scientist. Do you still understand what that means? I deal in *facts*. I'm not interested in all this mythology of yours. Now,

I've listened to what you've had to say, and I'm asking you to *go*! Go now, before you do something stupid.'

The old man gave an incoherent shout of rage.

Out of the corner of her eye, Holly saw someone come running towards the caravan across the grass. A young man, tall and solidly built with short dark hair and a tanned face.

'Anne!' called the young man. 'Are you all right?' He caught the professor by the shoulder, ducking as the walking-stick came sweeping through the air.

'Get your hands off me, you ruffian!' shouted Professor Rothwell.

Holly and her friends watched in shock as the young man snatched at the Professor's stick and wrenched it out of his hand.

'Christopher!' shouted the woman. 'Leave him. I can handle this.'

'Oh, my gosh!' breathed Holly as she saw the old professor stumble and fall heavily into the grass. She threw her bike down and ran between the Land-rovers, her three friends at her heels.

The fall seemed to have taken all the fight out of the old man. The young man was standing staring down at him, his mouth hanging open.

'I didn't touch him,' he said. 'Honestly. I didn't lay a finger on him.'

The woman ran down the steps, and with Holly and Tracy's help, they managed to get the old professor on to his feet. His pale blue eyes blazed in the cracked and wrinkled parchment of his face.

He pulled his walking-stick out of the young man's hands and glared round at them all, his hair as tangled as a bird's nest.

'You'll regret this,' he said, tugging his jacket straight. 'All of you. You'll regret that you ever came here.'

'I'm very sorry this happened,' said the woman. 'Are you all right? Can I give you a lift home?'

The old man drew away from them. He gave a dry laugh, like the cry of a crow. 'I don't need your help,' he said. 'It will be you in need of help if you stay here.' He stared at the woman. 'Do you think it's me you need to fear?' He pointed a shaking finger into the woman's face. 'Cernunnos will take revenge on you if you disturb his resting place.'

He pushed through the ring of people.

He stopped suddenly, his strange eyes fixing on Belinda. He reached for her and she backed away, alarmed by his expression.

'You should not be here, Epona,' he said to her. 'Of all people, you should not come here. Get away from this place.'

Belinda gave an embarrassed laugh and backed behind Kurt.

The old man's eyes swept over them again.

'Fools!' he growled.

They watched, dumbfounded, as he shambled

14

off across the grass and disappeared through the gate.

Holly let out a long, low whistle.

'Well,' she said. 'What was all *that* about?'

2 The legend of Hob's Mound

As they stood staring after the old man, they heard the wheezing growl of a car starting up. The battered brown car that they had seen parked by the hedge outside the field must have belonged to Professor Rothwell, Holly realised.

The woman gave a sigh, shaking her head.

'I could have done without that,' she said. She looked round at Holly and her friends. 'Thank you for helping,' she said. She frowned. 'Can I do anything for you?'

'My name's Kurt Welford,' said Kurt. 'I think my father arranged with you for me to take some photos.' He held his camera up. 'For the *Express*?'

The woman nodded. 'I hope you're not going to report this unfortunate incident to the newspaper,' she said. 'The less said about *that* the better.'

'But why was he so angry?' asked Holly.

The woman looked at her. 'Who are you?'

Holly introduced herself and her two friends, explaining about the article she hoped to write for the school magazine.

'I see,' said the woman. 'The press are gathering already.'

Holly felt a glow of pleasure at being described as 'the press'. Her biggest ambition was to become a journalist.

'I'm Anne Fairfax,' said the woman. 'I'm in charge of this dig. You're welcome to look round, so long as you don't get in the way.'

'Could you tell us why you're digging here now?' asked Holly, remembering what Kurt had told her about the previous excavation. 'Why now in particular?'

Anne Fairfax smiled. 'Some aerial photographs were recently taken of this area,' she said. 'When we put them through the computer it showed markings around the mound. Markings that proved the mound was once surrounded by a ring of standing stones. The stones are long gone, but the fact that they were here means that this was once an important grave site.' She smiled. 'Archaeology has come a long way in the past few years. We use a lot of modern technology nowadays, even though it's still down to careful spade-work in the end.'

Holly wrote this down in her notebook.

'What are you hoping to find?' she asked.

Anne Fairfax laughed. 'I'd rather not make wild guesses,' she said. 'Let's just say I'm very hopeful that there will be something important in there. Look, I'll be happy to give you an interview at some stage, but I've got some paperwork to catch up on.' She looked at the young man. 'I'm sure Christopher will show you everything. Will you do that for me, Christopher?' she asked. 'Answer their questions for me?'

The young man smiled. 'Sure,' he said, then frowning, 'I'm sorry about . . . you know.'

Anne Fairfax shrugged. 'Not to worry,' she said. 'Let's hope we've heard the last of him.' She mounted the steps to the caravan and closed the door behind her.

'I'm Chris Lambert,' said the young man. 'I'm a student of archaeology at the university.' He nodded over to where the other young people were watching them from the brown earth face of the dig. 'We're Professor Fairfax's team.'

'*Professor* Fairfax?' said Holly.

Chris nodded. 'She's one of the youngest professors of archaeology in the country,' he said. He gazed up at the closed caravan door. 'She's brilliant,' he said. 'Absolutely brilliant. What would you like to see?'

'Everything,' said Tracy. 'But I wish someone would explain what the problem was with that old man.' She looked round at Belinda. 'And what was that he called you?'

'I'm not sure,' said Belinda. 'It sounded like "pony". I think my mother's right; he's got a few slates missing.'

'He seems to have got pretty weird since he retired,' said Chris. 'You may not think it to see

18

him now, but he was a leading authority on Celtic archaeology in his day.' He led the four friends over towards the long hill. 'Do you know anything about the Celts?' he asked.

'Not much,' admitted Holly.

'It's fascinating stuff,' said Chris. 'Celtic civilisation covered most of Europe for over a thousand years.' He gestured towards the mound. 'We think this grave barrow dates from about 200 BC.'

'Wow!' said Tracy. 'That makes it over two thousand years old. That's incredible. What did you call it?'

'A barrow,' said Chris. 'The really important chieftains had these barrows built for them. Anne believes that we're going to find some amazing things in here.'

'What makes you think it won't already have been dug up in the past?' asked Holly, scribbling notes in her book. 'Surely after two thousand years, anything of value would already have been stolen?'

'That's where we might be in luck,' said Chris with a grin. 'You see, there's a legend that the place is haunted. We're hoping that will have kept people away in the past. And of course, as Anne just told you, no one realised how important this place might be until quite recently.'

Tracy gave a shiver. 'It isn't, is it? Haunted, I mean?'

Chris laughed. 'I don't believe in ghosts,' he

said. 'The only person haunting it that I can see is Professor Rothwell.'

'Can you tell us any more about him?' asked Holly. 'He seemed very put out about all this.'

'I don't know much about him,' said Chris. 'Except that he retired about ten years ago. The rumour at the university is that he got weirder and weirder until they had to get rid of him. He started off sane enough, but – I don't know – he got sort of hooked on the old legends, you know. He started believing all that mythological stuff about gods and curses and all that. When he got wind of this excavation he wrote a letter to the university, telling them that they shouldn't go anywhere near here.' Chris shook his head. 'And the next thing we know, he's turned up and he's started yelling at Anne like some kind of madman.' He looked sharply at Holly. 'Don't write any of this down,' he said. 'You heard what Anne said. The last thing she wants is to get tangled up with the ravings of some crazy old man.'

Reluctantly, Holly scribbled through Professor Rothwell's name. It seemed a shame not to be able to include the old professor in her article, but she could see Anne Fairfax's point.

'Is it OK for me to go round with my camera?' asked Kurt.

'Of course,' said Chris. 'Help yourself.'

While Kurt wandered off to take some photographs, Chris took the three girls over to where the other students from the university were carefully scraping away the layers of earth from the side of the barrow.

'Have you found anything yet?' asked Belinda.

'We're still only removing the outer layers,' said Chris as they watched the painstaking way the students peeled back the earth, examining every trowel-full before discarding it.

Tracy looked at the huge barrow, towering above them in the bright afternoon sunlight.

'Wouldn't it be quicker to use a mechanical excavator?' she said.

'Quicker,' said Chris with a laugh, 'but we'd probably destroy everything in the process. 'Archaeology is a very slow business, Tracy.' He smiled. 'Even with all the modern technology it's still down to hours and hours of patient digging, until we find those first traces of wood that mean we've hit on the burial chamber.'

'What do you expect to find inside?' asked Holly.

'If it is a chieftain, there'll be a funeral cart,' said Chris. 'Weapons, jewellery, ornaments.' He grinned. 'The Celts had very firm beliefs in the after-life, so they made sure their dead people had all the things they would need on their journey there. But I shouldn't get excited, if I were you. It'll be a few days yet before we work our way through to anything like that.'

'Could we come back?' asked Holly. 'Would that be all right?'

'You'll have to ask Anne about that,' said Chris. 'But I don't see why not. Who knows – maybe next time we might have something to show you.'

Holly, Belinda and Tracy sat in a circle on the grass in Holly's back garden, chatting about the dig at Hob's Mound and wondering what treasures Professor Fairfax might unearth.

'Did you notice how Chris called Professor Fairfax "Anne" all the time?' said Belinda. 'I'd have expected them to be a bit more formal than that. After all, he's only a student.'

Tracy grinned. 'Didn't you see the way he looked at her?' she said. 'I think there's something going on between those two.'

They could hear the sound of Mr Adams's lathe from his workshop in the garage. Since giving up his job as a solicitor when they had moved, he had put all his energies into his furniture-making business. Whilst Mrs Adams managed a branch of one of the local banks, her husband spent almost all his waking hours in his workshop.

'Do you think Professor Rothwell is really crazy?' asked Tracy. 'I mean, *really* crazy?'

'You heard what Chris said,' Holly pointed out. 'And you saw the way he was behaving up there.'

'I don't think he's crazy,' said Belinda. 'He's just a bit odd.' She glanced round. 'Jamie? What are you up to?'

Unnoticed by the three girls, Holly's little brother had come sidling up to them from the house.

'Nothing,' he said, all injured innocence.

'Haven't you got anything better to do than hang around annoying us?' said Holly. 'No matter what I do, you're always lurking about, listening.'

'I wasn't listening,' said Jamie. 'I'm not interested in some silly old digging. Not unless they were digging for fossils. You know, dinosaur bones.'

'Well, they're not,' said Holly. 'So you can stop eavesdropping and go and irritate someone else.'

Jamie stuck his tongue out at her and edged closer.

Holly looked suspiciously at him.

'You're up to something,' she said. 'I know you. What have you got hidden behind your back?'

'Nothing,' said Jamie.

'Show me!' said Holly, getting up and advancing on him. Jamie backed away, but she was too quick. She grabbed his arm and pulled it round.

'What's this then?' she said, prising his fingers loose from a small cardboard tub.

'Get off me,' said Jamie, struggling. 'It's mine.'

They fought over the tub. 'Itching powder!' she read. 'You little pest. I suppose this was meant for us, was it?'

'No! No!' yelled Jamie, half-shouting and half-laughing. 'I wasn't going to use it on you. I was just going to show it to you.'

Holly looked round at her friends. 'Want to help me teach him a lesson?' she said.

Belinda jumped up, trying to grab Jamie's arms. But he managed to jerk the tub out of Holly's grip just as Belinda came for him. The top sprang off and a spurt of grey powder landed on Belinda's hand.

Jamie gave a shriek of laughter as Belinda scratched at her hand.

'Got you!' he crowed.

'And now we'll get you,' said Holly, snatching the tub out of his hand and threatening to tip its contents over him.

As they fought a voice brought them to a sudden silence.

'What's all this racket?' Mr Adams was standing at his workshop door. 'I thought someone was being murdered.'

'Someone is!' said Holly. 'Him!'

Mr Adams calmed them down.

Belinda was scratching at her hand. The itching powder was certainly powerful stuff. She felt like she'd been attacked by a swarm of wasps.

Mr Adams frowned at Jamie. 'Leave your sister and her friends alone,' he said. He looked at Belinda. 'You'd better go inside and wash that stuff off,' he said. 'And you, Jamie, go and keep yourself out of mischief.'

'Can I dig in the garden?' asked Jamie. 'I want to find some fossils.'

'Yes, yes,' said Mr Adams. 'Anything to keep

24

you quiet.' He pointed down to the stretch of earth at the bottom of the garden. 'Dig down there,' he said. 'And when you get to Australia give me a shout.'

Jamie ran to get a spade and Mr Adams returned to his workshop.

'I hope he does get to Australia,' said Holly. 'I'll fill the hole in after him.' She pushed the tub of itching powder into her jacket pocket. The three of them went into the house and Belinda ran her hand under the tap.

'What were we talking about before Superpest arrived?' asked Holly.

'The Mad Professor,' said Tracy.

'Yes, well, never mind him,' said Holly. 'What I'd like to do is find out some more about the Celts. Some background for my article.'

'There might be something in the school library,' said Belinda, letting the cool water run over her hand.

Holly grinned at her. 'That,' she said, 'is a very good idea. Do you two fancy helping me tomorrow?'

Belinda looked at her. 'Do we have any choice?' she asked.

Holly laughed. 'Not really,' she said.

Belinda and Tracy knew Holly only too well. Once she had an idea in her head, the only thing they could do was follow in her wake.

* * *

'Look at my hand!' exclaimed Belinda. She had found Tracy and Holly in the school library at break the next day.

They were sitting over a pile of history books that they had taken down from the shelves.

They looked up as Belinda displayed her hand under their noses. There was an angry-looking rash where the itching powder had spilled on her the previous day.

'I'm going to kill that brother of yours,' said Belinda. 'I've hardly slept all night with it. That stuff should be illegal.'

'We can beat him up later,' said Holly. 'Look what Tracy and I have found.'

'I don't care what you've found,' said Belinda. 'I'm itching like mad.'

'Put some ointment on it,' said Tracy. 'And stop moaning!'

Belinda plumped down in a chair beside her two friends.

'That's what I like about you,' she said. 'You're so sympathetic.'

'We'll be sympathetic in a minute,' said Holly. She turned one of the books towards Belinda. 'Have a look at this.'

Grumbling to herself, Belinda looked at the open book.

All thoughts of her stinging hand were lost as she saw the words printed at the top of the page.

'*Epona*,' she read. '*Celtic horse goddess*.' She looked

up at them. 'Epona. That's what the Mad Professor called me yesterday.'

'That's right,' said Holly. 'And take a look at who wrote this book.'

Belinda turned the book over. '*Celtic Mythology*,' she read. '*An investigation into ancient legends by Lance Rothwell, Professor of European Archaeology.*' She stared at her friends. '*He* wrote this?'

'That's right,' said Tracy. 'It's dated twenty-five years ago. You see? He's been into this stuff for years.'

Holly nodded. 'So far into it, that it looks like he's lost touch with reality. Have a read of that piece about Epona, Belinda. I think it explains what all the fuss was about up at Hob's Mound.'

Belinda turned the book over again and began to read aloud.

'"It is told that in ancient days the horse goddess Epona tricked the horned god, Cernunnos, into a magic mound and bound him fast with sorcery so that he should never arise again to plague the world. For centuries Cernunnos has lain undisturbed, but should his resting-place be discovered, it is believed there is now no power in the world that could prevent his terrible revenge."'

Belinda blinked at her friends. 'And you think the Mad Professor *believes* all this?' she said. She shook her head. 'He can't,' she said. 'He can't be as barmy as all that, surely?'

'Are you sure?' said Tracy. 'You saw him. Holly

and I guess he thinks Hob's Mound is where Epona imprisoned this Cernunnos guy. That's why he freaked out when he heard they were going to dig there. He must think some whacky old god is going to come steaming out and kill everyone.'

'Crumbs,' breathed Belinda. 'Talk about out to lunch.' She closed the book, looking at her two friends. 'I'll tell you one thing,' she said. 'If I ever see that man again, I'm going to run for it. This is too creepy for words.'

'I think we should tell Anne Fairfax about this,' said Holly. 'When we go over there tomorrow. And meanwhile I'm going to see if I can read up some *real* Celtic stuff amongst this lot.' She looked at the collected pile of books. 'Some proper facts, not just a load of legends.'

'You do that,' said Belinda. 'I'm going to the sickroom to see if they've got any ointment for this rash.' She stood up. 'And then I'm going to kill Jamie. Slowly. Very slowly indeed.'

Belinda began the long walk up the hill that would take her home. She lived with her parents in a rambling, chalet-style house in the richest part of Willow Dale, although from looking at her, no one would guess her wealthy background. Her mother was always complaining about her appearance, unable to understand why Belinda chose to go about in an old green sweat-shirt and tatty jeans when she had a wardrobe full

28

of expensive clothes. Belinda ignored it. The only effort she took was over her horse, Meltdown, a chestnut thoroughbred.

Meltdown had his own stables at the bottom of the Hayes's immense garden, and as Belinda toiled up the slope on her way home from school that afternoon, she was already planning her evening ride.

She was so absorbed in these thoughts that she didn't even hear the coughing grumble of the car coming up behind her.

She jumped in surprise as the car halted at the kerb a few feet ahead of her. She recognised it with a nervous leap of her stomach. It was the car that had been parked on the grass verge near Hob's Mound the previous day. The brown car belonging to Professor Rothwell, the Mad Professor.

Belinda was no coward, but she couldn't prevent a tingle of unease running through her as the old professor got out of the car and turned to face her.

What had she said she would do if she ever saw him again? Run? But run where? He was between her and home.

She halted in her tracks, eyeing him warily as he leaned on his stick, staring at her.

A finger pointed towards her. 'I know you,' he said. His voice was quite calm, and the wild, angry look had gone from his face. He just looked old and tired.

'I don't think you do,' said Belinda, trying to keep her voice level.

'I've seen you,' he said, nodding. 'Riding down by the river. I know who you are. I know who you *really* are.'

'I'm sorry,' said Belinda. 'I've got to get home.' She moved towards him, pressing against the wall so as to keep as much distance between them as possible.

The old man looked searchingly into her face. 'I see,' he said. 'You're scared.' He nodded. 'You do well to be scared, but I can help you.'

'Look,' said Belinda. 'I'm sorry. I don't know what you're talking about. Can I get past, please?'

The old man laughed softly and drew something out of his pocket. 'Take this,' he said. 'It will protect you. Don't be frightened of me. I want to help you.'

Belinda looked at his outstretched hand. In his palm was a flat round stone with a hole. Looped through the hole was a leather thong.

'No, thanks,' said Belinda. 'I don't want it. I've never been keen on collecting stones.'

The old professor lurched forwards, catching Belinda's hand and pressing the stone into it.

'Take it,' he said. 'And stay away from Hob's Mound. They don't know the danger they're stirring up.'

Belinda stared at him. 'What danger?' she gasped. 'What do you mean?'

'When they open the mound, Cernunnos will be free,' said the professor. 'And he will take his revenge on you.'

'On *me*?' said Belinda. 'Why on me?'

A weird smile transformed the old man's face. 'Because you are Epona,' he said. 'You are the horse goddess who imprisoned him.' He nodded as Belinda stared at him in disbelief.

She trembled as the professor's wild eyes fixed on her.

'The stone will protect you,' he said. 'Wear it round your neck at all times. Be *warned*. They will try to take it from you. On no account must you let anyone take it.'

It seemed to Belinda that everything Holly and Tracy had suspected was true. The old man must be quite mad. She shivered as she looked into his face, terrified of what he might do next.

3 The goddess stone

The following morning Holly and Tracy were waiting impatiently by the school gates for Belinda to arrive. Belinda had telephoned them the previous evening, telling them about her strange encounter with Professor Rothwell, and of the stone he had thrust into her hand. They were dying with curiosity to see it.

By now Belinda had recovered from her fright. In fact, she had even started to feel sorry for the confused old man. After all, he had done her no harm. He had seemed genuinely worried for her, even if the reason for his concern was so outlandish. No sooner had he thrust the stone into her hand, than he had climbed back into his car and driven off.

As she came, wheeling her bike along the pavement, she was wearing the stone on its thong round her neck.

Her two friends ran up to her.

'Let's see it, then,' said Holly.

Belinda drew the thong up.

Tracy took the stone in her hand, turning it over.

It was light brown and quite smooth except for the hole through which the thong passed.

'What do you think it's supposed to be?' asked Tracy.

'How should I know?' said Belinda. 'He just said I should wear it to protect myself. I didn't feel like standing there chatting to him about it. He's not exactly Mr Normal, is he?'

'Don't you think we ought to do something about this mad professor of yours?' asked Tracy.

Belinda frowned at her. 'Like what?'

'Oh, I don't know,' Tracy said with a shrug. 'Tell the police he's hassling you? He might get violent.'

Belinda shook her head. 'I don't think he means any harm,' she said. 'He's just peculiar.' She gave Tracy a look. 'If I went about reporting peculiar people to the police, you'd have been locked up months ago.'

'Oh, thanks very much,' said Tracy. 'It takes one to know one.'

Holly laughed. 'Are you both up for a trip over to Hob's Mound after school?' she said. 'You never know, they might have found some treasure by now.'

'Or Cernunnos might have got out and murdered them all,' said Belinda.

'You're not beginning to believe all that, are you?' asked Tracy.

Belinda laughed. 'Of course not. Still, Holly's right, there might be *something* to look at.'

They walked with Belinda as she wheeled her bicycle over to the bike sheds.

'I just hope the Mad Professor doesn't turn up again,' Belinda said with an uneasy grin. 'I've had about as much weirdness as I can cope with for the time being.'

Things didn't seem much changed at Hob's Mound when the Mystery Club arrived that afternoon. The only difference was in the weather. The blue skies had given way to dark, threatening clouds, and there was already the odd drop of rain falling. The three girls rested their bicycles by the gate and walked over to where several young people were working at the earth face of the dig.

Chris was amongst them, his sleeves rolled up and his hands filthy from the soil. There was a heap of fresh brown earth on the grass and the scrape in the side of the mound was deeper. Progress was obviously being made, albeit with painstaking slowness. The other students were scooping earth up in trowels and picking carefully through it before casting it aside.

To one side a trestle-table had been set up. Anne Fairfax was leaning over the table, making notes on a clipboard.

'Hello,' called Holly. 'Is it OK for us to watch?'

'Of course,' said Chris, smiling and waving. He pointed to the table.

'We've found a few things,' he said.

Their eyes wide with anticipation, the three girls went over to the table. On one side lay a collection of small objects in labelled plastic bags. Anne Fairfax was writing something on another label.

'Any treasure yet?' asked Tracy.

Anne Fairfax smiled. 'Probably not your idea of treasure,' she said. She held up a small shard of brown pottery. 'Celtic origin,' she said. 'It's a good sign.' She slid the sliver of pottery into a plastic bag. 'It's like a jigsaw,' she said. 'We'll try to reassemble the pots from all these pieces.'

'But are they valuable?' asked Tracy.

'That depends,' said Anne Fairfax. 'To anyone involved in archaeology they're beyond price. We can learn an enormous amount from pieces like this.' She smiled. 'And there are private collectors who would pay a small fortune to get their hands on them. But these will all be going to a museum.'

She straightened her back with a sigh.

'Hello, what's this?' she said, catching sight of the stone round Belinda's neck. She leaned forwards for a closer look. 'Where did you get that?'

'Professor Rothwell gave it to me,' said Belinda. 'He said it would protect me.' She gave Anne Fairfax a puzzled smile. 'Do you know what it is, then?'

'It's a dobbie stone,' Anne said. 'The Celts used them to ward off evil. It's a sort of Celtic version of a rabbit's foot. A lucky charm. When did he give it to you?'

Belinda explained her brief encounter with the old man. Anne Fairfax shook her head.

'I feel so sorry for him,' she said. 'He had such a brilliant mind.'

The sound of a car revving through the gateway made them look round.

For an uncomfortable moment, Belinda thought it might be the old professor again, but it was a different car. It was a silver estate car. It came to a halt in the grass and a tall, hawk-faced man got out.

Pushing his hands into the pockets of his short khaki jacket, he walked over to the table. From Anne Fairfax's expression, Holly guessed she not only knew the man, but disliked him.

'What do you want, Mallory?' Anne Fairfax asked sharply.

The man smiled. 'Is that any way to greet a fellow enthusiast?' he said, unperturbed by the look on her face. He glanced over the table. 'Found anything interesting?'

'You're not welcome here,' said Anne Fairfax. 'I've said everything I have to say to you.'

The man smiled, picking up a piece from the scattering of pottery that had not yet been bagged. 'The offer still holds,' he said coolly, turning the piece in his fingers. 'My clients are prepared to pay top prices for anything worthwhile. You know how slowly the money appears if you go through the usual channels. I'm just trying to save you a bit of time.'

'And line your own pockets,' said Anne Fairfax. 'I've already made it clear to you – everything we find will go straight to a museum. So you and your private collectors will just have to look somewhere else.'

The man shook his head. 'It's a shame,' he said. 'Museums pay so poorly. Just think what you could do with the sort of money I'm offering?' He gave her a sly look. 'You could even fund that excavation in Brittany. The one the university doesn't seem willing to pay for.'

'How do you know about that?' said Anne Fairfax.

Mallory shrugged. 'I have my sources.' He looked over to the dig. 'Are you close yet?'

'I have *nothing* to say to you,' said Anne Fairfax, taking the piece out of Mallory's hand. 'I want you to leave. There's nothing here for you.'

'As you wish,' said Mallory, wiping his fingers on his jacket. 'You know where to contact me if you change your mind.' As he walked to the car, he looked back over his shoulder. 'I'll be waiting for your call.'

Holly and her friends stood silently to one side, puzzled by the encounter. Holly was disturbed by the anger in Anne Fairfax's face as she watched the car describe a wide circle in the grass and drive off through the gate.

'Who was that?' breathed Tracy.

Anne Fairfax frowned at her. 'No one,' she said. 'No one at all.'

Holly smiled, hoping to break the grim atmosphere that the man had left behind. 'Is there anything we can do here to help?' she asked.

'You could see if they've found any more pieces,' said Anne Fairfax. She looked down at the table. 'And I need some more bags. They're in the caravan, if you'd like to get them for me.'

'I'll go,' said Holly.

'Would you take these over for me as well?' asked Anne Fairfax, gathering up the bagged pieces and carefully loading them into Holly's arms. 'Just put them on the desk, will you?'

'And we'll go and see if Chris has dug up anything else,' said Belinda.

Holly went over to the caravan. Inside it looked like a particularly chaotic office. There was a small desk littered with papers. Piles of cardboard files leaned against the walls. Clothes and bags were heaped by the door.

I should have asked where the plastic bags were kept, Holly thought to herself, stepping over a collection of digging implements. Her foot caught on something and the bags slid out of her arms as she lost her balance and fell sprawling over the pile of clothes.

Holly lifted herself on to her knees, horrified that her fall might have damaged the pieces. Frowning, she looked down at what had caught her foot.

38

It was the strap of a red and white rucksack. She had tipped it over, sending its contents spilling out over the floor.

'Of all the clumsy idiots,' Holly hissed to herself. She gave a sigh of relief. As far as she could tell, she hadn't broken anything. The coats had cushioned the impact of the scattered bags.

'Oh, no! Jamie, I'll kill you!' She stared down at the grey powder that covered the plastic bags. Jamie's itching powder. She had completely forgotten the tub of the stuff in her pocket. She had meant to throw it away somewhere where her brother wouldn't be able to find it. The shock of her fall had jerked the tub out of her jacket pocket and the lid had come off.

Cautiously she lifted the tub in her fingertips, using its rim to gather as much of the powder as she could without actually touching it. She doubled over and blew the rest of the powder off the bags of discoveries.

'I hope that's got rid of it all,' Holly whispered to herself, getting to her feet. She picked up the bags one by one in her fingertips and placed them on the edge of the desk. It was amazing how trying to be helpful could cause so much trouble.

Holly crouched by the fallen rucksack. Lying half-out of the opening of the bag was something wrapped in a piece of cloth. She lifted it, surprised by its weight. It was only about twelve centimetres long, but very heavy. Like metal. A fold of the cloth came loose and she saw a flash of gold.

Holly battled with her natural curiosity. What was this heavy golden thing? She peeled the flap of disturbed cloth back. A golden head stared up at her. A man's head adorned with a pair of horns. The head of a golden statue.

There was a shout from outside. Holly glanced nervously towards the doorway, worried that someone might have seen her and think she was snooping.

But the shout was from way over at the dig.

Hurriedly she closed the cloth over the golden head and thrust the package back into the rucksack, pushing the other scattered things in after it.

Holly stood up, spotting the pile of empty plastic bags on top of a heap of filing boxes. Grabbing them, she ran down the steps.

Everyone was over at the dig. She could see Tracy jumping up and down with excitement.

Something had been found.

Holly ran to look.

Anne Fairfax was holding a flat grey stone across her open hands. It was square-shaped, no bigger than her palm. She seemed thrilled by it. Chris and the others were standing around her, their faces lit up with joy.

'A goddess stone,' said Anne Fairfax, all traces of her former anger gone. She wiped the dirt away

40

from the face of the stone. 'Look at the markings. This proves I was right all along. There's someone important buried in here.'

'What is it?' asked Holly.

'Proof that we're on the right track,' said Anne Fairfax. 'Something for you to mention in your article. The Celts buried these stones at the entrance to their tombs.'

Holly looked at the grooves scratched in the flat face of the stone. She couldn't make anything of them.

'What do the markings represent, Professor?' asked one of the students.

Anne Fairfax traced her fingers over the marks. 'This represents a horse,' she said. 'And these lines symbolise the horse goddess, Epona. Epona was one of their most powerful deities. They would only leave a goddess stone with the symbol of Epona here if the person buried inside was one of their most revered chieftains.' She hugged the stone against herself.

Belinda nudged Holly with her elbow. 'Epona again,' she said, staring at Holly.

'I'm going to take this straight to the university,' said Anne Fairfax. She looked up at the grey sky. 'It looks like we're in for some heavy rain,' she said. 'I think you'd better cover everything up for now.' She looked round at the others. 'Well done, all of you.'

*   *   *

41

Anne Fairfax had left in one of the Land-rovers. The other students tidied things up and spread a tarpaulin over the face of the dig. The rain was still threatening as the three girls walked over to their bikes.

'I wish they'd carried on digging,' said Tracy. 'I'm dying to see some proper treasures. I'm sure all these bits of stone are fascinating if you're an archaeologist, but it's not like finding jewels or gold, is it?'

'We need to talk,' said Holly. 'I've seen something that I can't quite make sense of.' She glanced round and became silent as she saw Chris approaching them.

'Seen what?' asked Belinda.

'Shush!' hissed Holly. 'I'll tell you later.'

'That was a bit of excitement, wasn't it?' said Chris. 'We should hit the burial chamber tomorrow, with any luck.'

'Aren't you afraid that someone might come along and dig it up overnight?' asked Holly.

'One of us always sleeps in the caravan,' said Chris. 'Look, if you aren't doing anything for the next half-hour, I could show you around. There are some fascinating things around here if you know where to look.'

'It's going to rain,' said Belinda. 'And anyway, I've spent half my life riding round here,' said Belinda. 'I probably know this area better than you do.'

Chris grinned. 'The rain should hold off for a little while,' he said. 'Do you know the Bloody Well?'

Belinda stared at him. 'The *what*?'

Chris laughed. 'I thought not. I've been studying this area really carefully. Come on, I'll show you. Leave your bikes. It's not far away.'

He led the three girls across the fields towards a low-lying patch of woodland.

'Do you know that man who was here earlier?' Holly asked him. 'Professor Fairfax didn't seem to think much of him.'

'John Mallory?' said Chris. 'Yes, I know him. He buys archaeological finds for private collectors. Rich people who lock the things away in vaults, when they should be on public display. I was surprised he had the nerve to show his face. He knows what Anne thinks of him. He must know he'll never get anything from her.' Chris frowned. 'I hope she keeps an eye on him, though. He'd love to discredit her and get her taken off the dig.'

'He mentioned another dig in Brittany,' said Belinda. 'What was that all about?'

'There's a major site waiting to be explored in France,' said Chris. 'But it's so expensive to set these excavations up. That's one of the reasons Anne is hoping for something big to come out of Hob's Mound. If she finds something important, the university will be more likely to give her the money to set up a foreign excavation.' He smiled.

'I'm really hoping it works for her. She's – she's a wonderful . . .' His voice trailed off. 'A brilliant scientist,' he finished with a sheepish smile.

Tracy gave Holly a wink behind Chris's back, tracing the shape of a heart in the air. 'You like her, don't you?' she said.

Chris gave her a startled look. 'What do you mean?'

Tracy shrugged. 'You sound as if you're fond of her, that's all.'

'There's nothing going on,' said Chris. 'If that's what you think. Nothing.'

'OK, OK,' said Tracy, surprised at the anxious tone in Chris's voice. 'I never said there was, did I?'

Chris smiled. 'Sorry,' he said. 'But I don't want anyone thinking there's anything between Anne and me. Professors aren't supposed to have personal relationships with their students.'

The three girls looked at one another, but didn't say anything. Chris couldn't have made it more obvious that there *was* something between him and Anne Fairfax if he'd tried. But as he obviously wanted it kept secret, Holly and her friends were quite happy to drop the subject.

'I hope this is going to be worth it,' said Belinda, as they forged their way through the thick woodland. 'If we get caught in the rain I'm going to be extremely annoyed.' A lithe branch whipped over her head. 'And I've always hated cross-country rambles.'

'We're almost there,' said Chris. 'Follow me.'

He led them deeper into the wooded hollow, until they came to an outcrop of rocky earth that loomed suddenly through the trees.

'This is it,' he said. 'Careful, the ground's quite marshy.' At their feet a stream of clear water bubbled downhill. The flood of sparkling water was coming out of a cleft low in the rock face.

'You've dragged us all this way to look at some water?' said Belinda. 'I can turn on a tap at home if I want to see water.'

'Not like this,' said Chris. 'It comes from an underground river. It feeds into the River Skelter. I was hoping it might be running red. It does that when there's been heavy rain. That's why it's called the Bloody Well. In the Middle Ages people thought it was a miracle. But it's actually caused by the river picking up red clay from somewhere under the hills.' He pointed through the trees. 'See how the land rises over there?' They looked over to the whale-backs of hills, barely visible through the branches.

'Those hills are riddled with caves,' he said. 'There's even a pothole that comes up on the hill above the well. I don't suppose any of you go potholing, do you?'

'I'd like to,' said Tracy. 'It's one of those things I've always wanted to do.'

'I shouldn't try it without expert help,' said Chris. 'It can be dangerous. You'd need proper equipment and a guide. It's like a maze. You could get lost in those caves for ever.'

'I'm tired, and I'm hungry,' interrupted Belinda. 'Have you got any more fascinating bits of water to show us, or can we go home now?'

Chris grinned apologetically. 'Sorry,' he said. 'I thought you might have been interested.'

'Take no notice of her,' said Holly. 'She's always complaining about something.' She looked at her watch. 'But I think we had better be getting back.'

They made their way to the field where Hob's Mound lifted its solitary hump.

Their bikes were where they had left them, leaning against the hedge, except that Tracy's bike had fallen over. She picked it up out of the grass.

'See you tomorrow,' shouted Chris as they cycled off. 'There should be plenty to look at.'

The three girls sat round Holly's kitchen table, Tracy and Belinda agog as Holly told them about the golden statue she had seen in the caravan.

'It can't be anything valuable,' Belinda pointed out after a few moments of thought. 'Or it wouldn't have been there. It's probably just a copy of something.'

'I suppose so,' Holly said with a sigh.

'If you're looking for mysteries,' said Belinda. 'It seems a lot more weird to me the way the name of this horse goddess, Epona, keeps cropping up.'

'You're not getting spooked, are you?' said Tracy.

'No . . .' Belinda said slowly. 'Not *spooked* exactly. But it is a bit creepy.'

Tracy laughed. 'Belinda's scared of ghosts!' she said. 'Now I've heard everything.'

'I'm not scared,' said Belinda.

'I bet you wouldn't go over to Hob's Mound at night, though,' said Tracy.

'I would if I could be bothered,' said Belinda. 'Why don't you, if you think it's such a good idea?'

'And what about Chris and Anne Fairfax?' said Holly. 'What do you think's going on there?'

Tracy laughed. 'I think he made that pretty obvious,' she said. 'They're having some kind of secret relationship.'

'I hope you're not planning on putting that in your article,' said Belinda. 'He might be the world's worst liar, but he's obviously trying to keep it a secret.'

'I'm not going to tell anyone,' said Holly. 'It's no business of ours. Anyway, I really like him, and Anne Fairfax.' She grinned. 'At this rate, this is going to be my best article ever. They've been really helpful to us, haven't they?'

The three friends spent the evening in Holly's room, chatting about the dig and helping Holly with her article.

It was twilight as Tracy cycled homewards. She was grinning to herself. *Belinda sure seemed jumpy,* she thought. *I bet she wouldn't go to Hob's Mound at night if you* paid *her!*

47

She looked down between the handlebars, intending to switch on the front lamp. But the lamp was missing from its plastic cradle.

Puzzled, she brought her bike to a halt.

'I *always* have my lights with me,' she said to herself. 'Oh, heck! Don't tell me I've lost it.' She thought back over the day, trying to guess what might have happened to it.

'It's at the dig!' she said, remembering how she had found her bike fallen in the grass. 'It must have come off then.'

It would take her only ten minutes or so to cycle over to the field and retrieve her lamp.

It's a good thing I don't believe in ghosts, thought Tracy as she headed for Hob's Mound in the half light. *A person could get really spooked with all these shadows.*

She had to admit that things did look a lot more mysterious in the rapidly fading light. It was eerily quiet as she cycled along the country road and saw the black shape of Hob's Mound looming over the bushes.

Tracy came to the gate. The field was a sea of dark shadows. She peered into the gloom. Hob's Mound was a wall of impenetrable blackness. She got off her bike and let herself in through the gate. She hardly had to search; the white shape of her lamp was lying in the grass under the hedge. Picking it up, she turned to leave.

Tracy caught her breath. Bobbing and dancing

at the base of Hob's Mound was a ghostly yellow light!

As she stood petrified, the light seemed to come wavering towards her, and she heard a low, trembling groan.

Tracy swallowed, her eyes round with fright. Could it really be true? Was Hob's Mound haunted after all?

Tendrils of fear came creeping up Tracy's legs as the eerie yellow light glided through the darkness towards her.

A low, chilling laugh drifted across the field.

It was too much. Tracy ran to the gate and jumped on to her bike. She spun her bike round and pedalled as fast as she could for the safety of the town.

'There are no ghosts. There *are* no ghosts!' she panted as the wheels spun. She took a few moments to push her lamp into its cradle between her handlebars and switch it on. The gleam of her headlamp skittered across the bushes, a feeble companion in all that gathering darkness.

Tracy felt the sweat trickling down between her shoulder-blades as she saw the comforting lights of the town. She would be home in a few minutes now. Safe at home.

And she had laughed about *Belinda* getting spooked!

4   Buried treasure!

In the cold light of day, Tracy felt like kicking herself for the way she'd reacted. She wasn't a six-year-old. Why had she let her imagination run riot like that?

Her mother was already up and getting ready to head off for the nursery she ran when Tracy came in, nibbling at a slice of toast.

Mrs Foster gave her a surprised look, seeing that Tracy was in her running shorts and ready to leave.

'You're early,' she said. 'What's wrong? Couldn't you sleep? Or are you in training for a marathon now?' Tracy always went for a morning run, but never quite this early.

'I slept fine,' said Tracy, not entirely truthfully. 'I just felt like taking a longer run this morning.'

'Don't wear yourself out,' said Mrs Foster with a smile. 'You don't always have to be breaking records.'

Tracy smiled. 'I won't,' she said. 'Don't worry.'

Tracy skipped out on to the pavement, but instead of her usual early-morning route through

50

the back streets, she set off at a steady jog towards Hob's Mound.

The clouds were still hanging over the town, but as yet there hadn't been more than a few scattered drops of rain to cool the early morning air.

This was the only way she could think of to banish the fears that had sent her racing her bike home the previous evening. Go back to Hob's Mound and see for herself that there was nothing spooky or sinister about the place.

She jogged easily up the long sloping road between the fields, taking deep, slow breaths, enjoying herself in the still of the early morning. She came to a halt at the gate. The grey square of the caravan stood alone in the dewy grass. No one had arrived yet to start the day's digging. Hob's Mound reared innocently in the field.

'You see?' said Tracy to herself. 'It's just a hill. Nothing to be afraid of.'

As she looked, the door of the caravan opened and Chris Lambert came down the steps, yawning and stretching.

He caught sight of her and waved.

She waved back and waited as he came over to her.

'You're a bit early,' he said, smiling. 'There won't be anyone else here for an hour or so.' He looked at her running kit. 'Or are you just passing?'

'Well, no, not really,' Tracy admitted. 'Have you been here all night?'

51

Chris nodded. 'I told you,' he said. 'Someone always sleeps here. It was my turn last night.'

'You didn't hear anything strange last night, did you?' Tracy asked cautiously.

'What kind of strange?' asked Chris.

'I don't know,' said Tracy. She told Chris of her late evening visit to Hob's Mound, and of the light and the weird noises.

Chris laughed. 'I think you've let the old legends get to you,' he said. 'You sound like you think you saw some ghosts.'

Tracy shook her head. 'I don't believe in ghosts,' she said.

'Then you must have imagined it,' said Chris.

'No,' said Tracy. 'I saw *something*.'

'Look,' said Chris. 'If there had been anyone up here, I'd have heard them.' He looked closely at her. 'There was no one here apart from me, I promise. And I wasn't wandering about with a light, I can tell you that much.'

'So what did I see?' asked Tracy.

Chris looked thoughtful. 'You don't think the old man was right, do you?' he said. 'You don't think Hob's Mound could really be haunted? The legends of the lights on Hob's Mound go back centuries, you know.'

'You don't believe that, do you?' asked Tracy.

Chris shrugged. 'You tell me,' he said. 'It was you who saw the light and heard – what was it – moaning?'

'Moaning and creepy laughing,' said Tracy. 'And it was coming towards me. Like it was trying to scare me off.'

Chris whistled softly. 'That's really strange,' he said. 'I can't explain it.'

'No,' said Tracy softly. 'Neither can I.' She smiled. 'Maybe I did imagine it all. Belinda and I were trying to scare each other with ghost stories. I guess I just let my mind play tricks on me.' She turned and looked back down the hill. 'I'd better be getting home,' she said. 'I don't want to be late for school.'

'I think it was probably the wind you heard,' said Chris. 'And maybe you just imagined the light?' He looked uneasily at her. 'Either that, or the place really is haunted.'

'Now I've gotten you spooked,' said Tracy with a laugh.

'I'm not spooked,' said Chris with a grin. 'But I'll keep my eyes open next time I spend the night here. Just in case.'

Tracy jogged back to the town. She showered and changed into her school clothes before heading off on her bike.

She found Holly and Belinda in their classroom.

Tracy told them about the previous night, trying to make it sound very matter-of-fact, leaving out any mention of her panic attack.

'Chris was there this morning,' she told them. 'He said there couldn't have been anyone there last night. I guess the light I saw was just some kind of reflection or something. And the noises were just the wind.'

'You don't suppose Professor Rothwell could have been doing it?' asked Holly. 'You know what he's like about the place. He could be pretending to be a ghost to frighten people off. To try and get the dig stopped.' Her eyes lit up with a new thought. 'Or what if he isn't as crazy as he sounds? What if he's got some other reason for wanting people to stay away from there?'

'You mean he wants to frighten everyone off and get the stuff for himself?' said Belinda. She shook her head. 'I don't think so,' she said. 'I think he really believes all those legends.'

'I don't know who or *what* it was,' said Tracy. 'But I'm not going up there at night again, that's for sure.'

Belinda grinned at her. 'Did you think the ghoulies were going to get you? I bet you were scared silly. Go on, admit it.'

'No way,' said Tracy. 'And anyway, if you're so sure it's all nonsense, how come you're still wearing that stone round your neck?'

Belinda laughed. 'Because I like it,' she said. 'I'm certainly not wearing it to protect myself against ghosts. Besides, it drives my mother crazy and that's reason enough to keep wearing it.'

'Are we going over to Hob's Mound after school?' asked Holly.

'I am,' said Belinda with a grin. 'But Tracy might not want to risk it. The ghosts might come back for her.'

'For the last time,' Tracy said in exasperation, 'I don't believe in ghosts. And I was *not* scared.'

'We believe you,' said Holly with a laugh. 'Thousands wouldn't, but we do. But I'll tell you where I do want to go this afternoon. To the museum. One of those books I got out of the school library mentioned something about a place called Elfbolt Hill, about thirty-five kilometres away from here. Another Celtic barrow. They found a whole load of things in there, years ago. It's all on display in the museum. I'd like to take a look at that.'

'I thought we were going straight over to Hob's Mound?' said Belinda.

'We'll have time to do both,' said Holly. 'But the museum closes early, so I'd like to go there first. You don't have to come if you don't want to.'

'We'll come,' said Belinda. 'Then we'll go over to the dig. And then we'll see if there really is anything in there.'

The Willow Dale Museum was a small greystone building in the square behind the church, in the unspoilt old centre of the town. It was just three or four medium-sized rooms, mostly filled with local artefacts and information about the town in the old days.

The three girls chained their bikes up to the

railings outside and walked up the broad steps to the entrance lobby. An elderly woman sat knitting behind a desk on which were piled postcards and guide-books. Beyond a wide arch, they could see rooms leading into one another, filled with display cabinets.

'Excuse me,' said Holly. 'Can you tell us where the things from Elfbolt Hill are displayed?'

The woman looked up from her knitting. 'The Celtic artefacts?' she said. 'Oh, dear. Have you come here especially to see them?'

Holly frowned. 'Aren't they here?'

'Yes, they're *here*,' said the woman. 'But I'm afraid you won't be able to see them at the moment.'

'Has something happened to them?' asked Tracy.

'Oh, no. Nothing like that,' said the woman. 'They're just not on display for the time being. Some students from the university have been using them for research. They're locked away in the workroom.' The woman smiled. 'If you could come back next week, I'm sure they'll be back on display by then.'

The woman saw the disappointment on the girls' faces.

'Was it important?' she asked.

'I'm writing a piece for our school magazine,' explained Holly. 'Next week will be too late.'

The woman lifted a guide-book from the pile and flipped through the pages. 'There are some good photos in here,' she said, 'if that's any use to you.' She spread the booklet out in front of them. The girls leaned over the table to look.

Holly's eyes widened. Amongst the photographs of bronze belt buckles and bracelets and brooches, one picture jumped up at her. A golden statue. A statue of a standing man. And rising from the man's head were a pair of horns.

It was an exact replica of the golden head she had seen sticking out of the cloth in the caravan at Hob's Mound.

'What size would this be?' Holly asked the woman, pointing at the photograph.

'Oh, not very big,' said the woman. 'It gives you all the details underneath.'

Holly scanned the writing beneath the photograph.

'Golden statue of the horned god Cernunnos. Celtic origin. Circa 200 BC. 14cms in height. Found by Professor L Rothwell at Elfbolt Hill, Yorkshire.'

Holly's mouth dropped open. 'Professor Rothwell found this?' She gaped at the woman. 'The Professor Rothwell who lives here?'

'I believe he still lives locally,' said the woman. 'You know of him, then?'

'Do we *know* of him?' breathed Tracy. 'I'll say.'

'I think he's something of a recluse these days,' said the woman. 'He used to come here on occasion, but I haven't seen anything of him for a year or two.'

'Are you absolutely certain that this statue is here?' asked Holly. 'It couldn't have gone missing, could it?'

The woman gave her a puzzled look. 'Of course it's here,' she said. 'I saw it myself, this morning. It's locked up in the workroom. What makes you ask?'

'I thought I saw something like it,' Holly said cautiously. 'Is this the only one of its kind?'

'There's a similar statue in a museum in Edinburgh,' said the woman. 'And several like it on the Continent. But this is the only one found so far in this part of the country.'

'Thanks,' said Holly. 'Thanks very much. I think we'd better be going.' She bundled Belinda and Tracy out on to the steps.

'It's the same as the one I saw in Professor Fairfax's caravan,' Holly said excitedly. 'I'm *sure* it is.'

Belinda shrugged. 'You heard what the woman said. The real one's locked up back there. You must have seen some kind of copy.'

Holly frowned. 'I suppose so,' she said. 'But it's funny that it was Professor Rothwell who found the stuff at Elfbolt Hill. Perhaps he started going peculiar after taking the things out of the barrow there.' She stared at her friends. 'Perhaps something *happened* to him there?'

'Like what?' mocked Tracy. 'Like some kind of curse? Get real, Holly. The guy's a flake, that's all.'

'Can we go over to Hob's Mound now?' asked Belinda. 'We could be missing all the fun, standing here arguing.'

They unchained their bikes. As they wheeled them to the kerb, they heard footsteps approach and stop behind them.

'Well, well. We meet again.' They looked round.

It was the hawk-faced man that Anne Fairfax had sent away from the dig the previous day. John Mallory. The dealer with the rich clients.

He smiled. 'You don't remember me?'

'We remember you, OK,' said Tracy.

'Have you been over to Hob's Mound recently?' he asked, seemingly unconcerned by their cold looks. 'I hear they're close to a big find.'

'I couldn't tell you,' said Holly warily.

He nodded. 'Ah . . .' he said. 'I see Professor Fairfax has been telling you tales about me. I shouldn't believe all you hear, if I were you.'

'We'll mention that to her,' said Tracy. 'We're going over there now. They're expecting to reach the tomb today.'

'Tracy!' hissed Holly.

Mallory's eyebrows raised. 'Really?' he said. 'I didn't realise they were so close. Thanks for letting me know.' He smiled round at them. A look of interest came over his face as he spotted the stone hanging round Belinda's neck. He leaned closer.

'Where did you get that?' he asked.

'It was a present,' said Belinda.

'You don't say?' he murmured. 'Do you know what it is?'

'Yes, I do, thanks,' said Belinda. She looked at the others. 'Shall we go?'

'I know people who would pay quite a nice price for a piece like that,' said Mallory, ignoring the abrupt tone in Belinda's voice.

'Sorry,' said Belinda. 'It's not for sale.'

Mallory straightened up. 'As you wish,' he said. He nodded to them and walked briskly away.

'You goon!' Holly exclaimed, glaring at Tracy. 'Why did you go and tell him about them getting into the tomb today? That's just what he was trying to find out.'

'Don't yell at me,' said Tracy. 'He'd have found out sooner or later, wouldn't he?'

'Well, if he's up there when we arrive, we'll know who to thank,' said Belinda. 'Motormouth Foster, again.'

'Never mind about that,' said Tracy. 'Don't you realise? He was trying to get the stone off you.'

'So?' said Belinda. 'He sells stuff like that. What's the big deal?'

'Didn't you say that the Mad Professor told you someone would try to take it off you?' said Tracy. 'And that's exactly what Mallory was trying to do. Don't you think that's a bit weird?'

'He didn't try to *take* it,' said Belinda. 'He wanted to buy it. And he didn't exactly put much pressure on to get it from me, did he? It's a coincidence,

Tracy. Or are you beginning to believe old man Rothwell can see into the future?'

'I didn't say that,' Tracy said sullenly. 'It's odd, that's all.'

'Shall we go?' said Holly. 'I want to stop off home on the way, and let them know I'll be a bit late.' She wheeled her bike to the kerb. 'Come on,' she said. 'To the treasure!'

They parked their bikes outside the front door of Holly's cottage. There was scaffolding against the side wall and a couple of men were doing something up amongst the chimney-pots.

'Aren't they ever going to finish this place?' asked Tracy. The Adamses' cottage had been under siege from workmen ever since they had arrived in Willow Dale. The renovations had been going on for months.

'I don't ask any more,' sighed Holly. 'Mum goes a sort of sickly green if I even mention it.'

They were just heading up the path when Jamie came haring out of the front door, brandishing a chunk of grubby white china.

'Look what I've found!' he shouted. 'I was digging, and I found this. It was a couple of feet down. I bet it's really old.'

Holly jerked her head back as he waved the piece of china under her nose. 'I bet you it's Roman, at least,' he crowed. 'I'm going to sell it to the museum.'

61

Holly grabbed it out of his hand. 'Roman!' she scoffed, wiping earth off it. 'You really do live in a world of your own, don't you? Look!' She held the china up to his eyes. 'It's just a bit of an old plate. It's even got "Made in Birmingham" written on it!'

The girls laughed and Jamie's face went red. 'Well?' he said. 'The Roman's might have made stuff in Birmingham. Why shouldn't they?'

'Because Birmingham probably didn't exist in Roman times,' laughed Belinda. 'And even if it did, it would have been called something else.'

'Better luck next time,' said Tracy. Jamie scowled, snatching the piece of plate out of Holly's hand and flinging it into the bushes.

'Is Dad home?' asked Holly.

'No,' said Jamie. 'He's gone to deliver some stuff. And you had a phone call about half an hour ago. From Tracy's boyfriend.'

'Kurt?' said Tracy. 'What did he want?'

'He said to tell you to get over to the dig as soon as you can,' said Jamie.

'They must have found something,' said Tracy. 'Come on, you guys, let's get over there.'

They left Jamie staring sulkily after them as they headed at full speed over to Hob's Mound to find out what Professor Fairfax and her team had dug out of the ancient Celtic barrow.

There were several cars parked on the verge outside

the gate, and a small crowd of people over by Hob's Mound.

The three girls ran across the field, desperate to see what was going on. There must have been more than a dozen people there. Some were shouting questions while others took photographs.

Through the gaps in the small scrum of people, Holly could see Anne Fairfax standing at the centre of attention, holding something high in her hands. Something that flashed in the sunlight.

Holly came to a skidding halt, her mouth falling open.

'What?' panted Belinda, bumping into her. 'What is it?'

'It's a gold statue,' breathed Holly.

'Wow!' gasped Tracy. 'They've really found something!'

'But don't you see?' whispered Holly, staring at her two friends. 'It's exactly the same as the one we saw in the museum guide-book. And *exactly* the same as the one that fell out of the rucksack.' She pulled her friends back from the crowd.

'Are you sure?' said Belinda. 'It can't be.'

'It is,' said Holly. 'And you know what that means, don't you? It means this whole thing is a *fake*!'

5 Deception

The three girls stared dumbly through the crowd. Anne Fairfax was wreathed in smiles, lifting the golden statue for the photographers, like an athlete holding up a trophy.

Holly's revelation had rooted them to the spot. Could she possibly be right? Was the glittering statue in Anne Fairfax's hands a fake?

'What are you going to do?' breathed Belinda.

'I don't know,' said Holly. She looked anxiously at her friends. 'I *could* be wrong,' she said.

'You said you were certain,' said Tracy. 'And it sure looks like the statue in the photo.'

'I know, I know,' said Holly. 'But how can I be sure it's the one I saw in the rucksack? I can't just march up there in front of all these people and accuse her of being a liar.'

'You've got to do something,' said Tracy. 'If this whole thing's a fraud, they've got to be told.' She gave Holly a push. 'Go on,' she said. 'Say something.'

Reluctantly, Holly walked forwards, edging her way through the circle of people. She saw Chris standing next to Anne Fairfax, grinning from ear to ear, gazing at her as if he thought she was the most wonderful person in the world.

Kurt was there as well, clicking away with his camera.

It looked as though the find had brought out reporters and photographers from every newspaper in the county. Questions were being shot at Anne Fairfax from every side.

Holly pushed her way to the front.

'Professor Fairfax,' she shouted. 'Wasn't there a statue very like this one found near here a few years ago?'

Anne Fairfax turned, hearing Holly's voice above the general noise.

'That's absolutely correct,' she said. 'It was discovered by Professor Rothwell only thirty miles from here.'

'Isn't it a bit unusual to find two statues so close to each other?' asked Holly.

Anne Fairfax's smile faded slightly. 'Unusual, certainly,' she said. 'But not unheard of. This grave barrow dates from the same time as Elfbolt Hill, where the other piece was found. There's no reason why grave offerings from the same period shouldn't be similar. The various Celtic tribes would all have worshipped the same gods.'

There was a disturbance from the other side of the crowd as someone pushed his way roughly to the front.

It was John Mallory. He stood looking at Anne Fairfax with narrowed eyes, his hands thrust deep in his pockets.

'If there are no more questions,' said Anne Fairfax, 'I think it's time this wonderful piece was taken off to the university for proper authentication. Thank you all for coming. I promise that you will be kept informed of all further developments.'

'One moment,' barked Mallory. 'You say it is not unheard of for statues of a similar design to be found near one another?'

'That's correct,' Anne Fairfax said sharply.

Mallory smiled. 'Neither is it unheard of for archaeologists anxious to enhance their reputations to, shall we say, *misrepresent* their findings.'

Anne Fairfax's eyes blazed. 'What do you mean by that?'

Holly was dumbfounded. It sounded as if John Mallory was as suspicious of the golden statue as she was.

'I mean,' declared Mallory, as all faces turned to look at him. 'I mean that an archaeologist in desperate need of funds to mount an excavation in Brittany might consider faking a discovery in the hope of raising the money.'

'How dare you!' shouted Anne Fairfax, as a murmur of voices rose around John Mallory's comment.

Holly saw Chris spring towards Mallory, a look of pure hatred on his face.

'Christopher!' shouted Anne Fairfax, catching the young man by the arm. 'Leave him! He only wants to cause trouble.'

'Professor?' called one of the reporters. 'Do you have an answer to these accusations?'

'I've already told you the facts,' said Anne Fairfax, bright spots of colour highlighting her cheeks. 'The statue was found here this afternoon, by Christopher Lambert, one of my students. It has been cleaned for your photographs, and will be taken straight from here to the university, where it will be properly authenticated.' She strode towards Mallory, holding the statue up to his face. 'Look at it!' she said. 'Do you see any sign of it being a fake?'

Holly held her breath as Mallory took the statue out of Anne Fairfax's hands. He turned it in his fingers, examining it closely.

He gave her a long, hard stare.

'It seems to be genuine,' he said slowly, handing it back to her. 'I shall await the official report with interest.' He turned and shoved his way out of the crowd.

'Apologise!' shouted Chris as Mallory walked away towards the gate. 'Apologise to the professor!'

'Let it be,' said Anne Fairfax. 'He can't do us any harm.' She cradled the statue in her hands, smiling again. 'We mustn't let the likes of him spoil the day.'

The crowd began to disperse, the reporters and photographers wending their way back to their cars. Belinda gave Holly a shove with her elbow.

'It's a good job you kept quiet,' whispered Belinda. 'It looks like you've got it all wrong. If *he* reckons it's the real thing, then it *must* be. He'd be the first person to shout about it if it were a fake.'

Holly watched as Anne Fairfax climbed into her Land-rover. She wound down the window and Holly saw Chris lean forwards to speak to her. Holly didn't hear what passed between them, but she did see Anne Fairfax's hand come out of the open window to give Chris's arm an affectionate squeeze.

So it is *true*, thought Holly. *There really is something going on between them, just like we thought.*

Anne Fairfax wound the window up and drove out of the gate, Chris gazing after her.

The business with the statue was a puzzle, Holly had to admit. But she was a lot slower to admit that she was completely wrong, no matter what John Mallory had said at the end.

The three girls sat in a circle on Holly's bed amidst the debris of an evening snack. Belinda and Tracy were becoming irritated by Holly's stubborn refusal to abandon her theories about the golden statue.

The Mystery Club's, red notebook was open in her lap. The name of Professor Anne Fairfax was written out in capitals with a large question mark after it.

'Why won't you just admit you got it wrong?' said Belinda.

Holly shook her head. 'Because I haven't,' said Holly. 'I don't care what you think. You two didn't see the statue in the caravan. *I* did. It was the same one.'

'It *can't* be,' Tracy said in exasperation. 'You heard what the professor said. They dug it up this afternoon. Even that guy Mallory had to admit it was the real thing.'

'That's not what he said,' Holly argued. 'He said it *seemed* to be genuine. Of course it would have to *look* genuine. Professor Fairfax wouldn't be so stupid as to show people something that looked like a fake.'

'But why would she fake it?' insisted Belinda.

'We know why,' said Holly. 'Chris told us. If she finds something important at Hob's Mound, the university will be prepared to give her the money to go to this other dig in France. And Mallory said the same thing.'

'Mallory was just being malicious because she wouldn't let him have any of the stuff they found,' said Tracy. 'That's obvious.'

'There is *one* way of proving whether you're right or not,' said Belinda. 'That statue can't be in two places at once, can it?'

Holly gave her a puzzled look.

'Don't you see?' said Belinda. 'All you've got to do is find some way of getting back into that caravan again and have another look in the rucksack. If that statue you saw is still in there, then you're wrong.'

'And if it isn't?' Holly said excitedly. 'Will you two start believing me?'

Tracy and Belinda looked at each other.

'I guess so,' said Tracy. 'But if you're right, it's not just the professor, is it? All the other people in the team must be in on it as well.'

'Not necessarily,' said Holly. 'She could have planted it when there was no one else there. She could have gone up there in the evening. She could have dug a hole, stuffed the statue in there, filled the hole in again, and the next morning when they start digging – wham! There it is! Instant treasure. And no one else would suspect a thing.'

'The light!' said Tracy. 'The light I saw there last night! That could have been someone burying the statue. And they'd have seen me. They could have pretended to be ghosts or something to frighten me off.'

'Are you sure it's that easy to bury something so that other people would believe it had been there all along?' said Belinda.

'Of course,' said Holly. 'And I can prove it to you.' She scrambled off the bed.

'Now what?' asked Belinda, as Holly opened a

70

drawer in her bedside cabinet and began rummaging around.

'There!' Holly turned, displaying a handful of foreign coins. 'These were left over from our holiday in Germany last year,' she said. 'I'm going to bury them at the bottom of Jamie's hole. You'll see. He's bound to have another dig around in there tomorrow. And I bet you he'll think they've been there for years.'

Belinda laughed. 'It doesn't take much to fool Jamie,' she said. 'He's not exactly a student of archaeology. Pest-ology, maybe.'

'Perhaps you're right,' said Holly. 'But I still think that's what happened, even if it isn't worth trying my theory out on Jamie.'

Belinda grinned. 'I still think you should bury them for him,' she said. 'It'll be revenge for his trick with the itching powder if we get him to think he's found something really valuable. I'll enjoy telling him he's been conned.'

'Meanwhile,' said Tracy, 'how are you going to get yourself another look at that rucksack? That's where the *real* proof is going to be.'

'Tomorrow's Saturday,' said Holly. 'We can go over to Hob's Mound in the morning. We can offer to help again. It worked last time. That's how I got into the caravan in the first place. We'll make ourselves useful, and the first chance I get, I'll go back in there and look in the rucksack.'

71

'Are you sure we should do that?' asked Belinda. 'It seems a bit underhand to me.'

'Not as underhand as trying to con people into believing you've found some ancient treasure,' said Holly. 'It's not as if I'm going to take anything.' She went to the door. 'And now,' she said, 'while Jamie's playing his computer games, I'll just creep off into the garden and plant a bit of fake treasure for *him* to find.'

The girls were in for a surprise when they arrived at Hob's Mound the next morning. A strange car was parked in the road, and someone had put a padlock and chain on the gate that led to the field.

They leaned over the gate. The field was deserted. The Land-rovers were gone.

'That's odd,' said Holly. 'I'd have thought they'd be here by now.' She looked over towards the caravan. 'What do you think can have happened?'

'Perhaps they're having a lie-in,' suggested Belinda. 'That's what I wanted to do this morning.'

'I wouldn't have thought so,' said Holly.

'Let's go see,' said Tracy, climbing on to the gate. She swung her leg over, giving Holly a quizzical look. 'You never know,' she said. 'This could be your big chance if they haven't locked the caravan up.'

The long grass left wet streaks on their shoes as

the three girls made their way over to the caravan. There was no sign of any work having been done at the dig that morning.

'It's bound to be locked,' said Belinda. But as they drew nearer they could all see that the door to the caravan was slightly ajar.

'What did I tell you?' said Tracy with a grin.

Belinda looked nervously around. 'I don't like this,' she said. 'I feel like a criminal.'

'We're not criminals,' said Holly. 'We're the Mystery Club.' She was about to step up to the door when it was pulled open from the inside.

Holly gave a shocked gasp. A man she had never seen before was standing in the doorway, staring down at her.

'How did you get in here?' he demanded, staring down at the three startled girls.

'We were looking for Professor Fairfax,' said Holly, recovering from her surprise. 'We thought she might let us help again.'

'It's OK,' added Tracy. 'She knows us. We've helped out up here before.'

The man frowned down at them. 'Didn't it occur to you that the gate was locked to stop people getting in here?' he said.

Holly gave him a hopeful smile. 'We only wanted to help,' she said.

'There's nothing going on here today,' said the man.

'Why not?' asked Tracy. 'I'd have thought they'd be digging away like crazy after yesterday.'

'There's been a break-in,' said the man. 'Someone busted their way in here early this morning. I've been sent over by the university to keep watch until the police arrive.'

'A break-in?' gasped Holly. 'Was anything taken?'

'They got away with some bags of stuff, apparently,' said the man.

'And the statue?' said Tracy. 'Did they get that?'

The man shook his head. 'That's over at the university.'

'But I thought someone slept here at night,' said Holly. 'They weren't hurt, were they?'

'No. The thieves timed it just right,' said the man. 'One of the lads, Chris Lambert, was here overnight. They must have waited until they saw him leave first thing. They only had about an hour, while he went to get some fresh clothes.' He folded his arms. 'There's no point in you three hanging around,' he said. 'Like I told you, there's nothing going on here until the police have been. The other students have been sent home and Professor Fairfax is over at the university.'

Stunned by the man's news, the three girls walked back towards the gate.

'What do you make of that?' said Tracy.

'Someone was after the statue, I reckon,' said

Belinda. 'I mean, enough people knew they'd found it. It's lucky for Chris that they waited until he'd left.'

'But where does that leave us?' said Holly. 'We're never going to get in there for a look in that rucksack now. Not after this.'

'You're just going to have to think of some other way of finding out whether the professor is a con artist,' said Tracy.

'Like how?' asked Holly. 'We can't just go up to her and ask about what she's got hidden in her rucksack.'

'Why not ask Chris?' said Belinda. 'Perhaps he knew about the statue in the rucksack. He might be able to tell us what it is – you know, explain why it was there.'

'I *know* why it was there,' said Holly. 'So she could pretend to have found it.'

'Not necessarily,' said Belinda. 'Not if the one they dug up was real and the one in the rucksack was just some copy.'

'Why should she have a copy, though?' asked Tracy.

'I don't know,' said Belinda. 'That's what we're trying to find out, isn't it?'

'But Chris won't tell *us* anything that might incriminate Professor Fairfax,' said Holly. 'Even if he knows what's been going on.'

'What you *think* has been going on,' Belinda reminded her. 'We've got no proof yet. I still think there could be some perfectly reasonable explanation. We can't be sure of *what* you saw in the caravan.'

'*I'm* sure,' said Holly.

'OK,' said Belinda. 'You're sure. But I'm not. I know you and your imagination, and I'm not going to believe this was all a hoax until we find out a bit more about exactly what was in that rucksack. And the best way of finding that out, if you ask me, is to have a word with Chris. We needn't let on we suspect anything.'

'And if he denies all knowledge of any statue being hidden in the caravan?' asked Holly. 'Then what?'

'Then,' said Belinda, 'I'll start believing there's something fishy going on.'

Holly nodded. Belinda was right. If there was nothing suspicious about the statue in the rucksack, Chris would surely have known it was there. He'd also be able to tell them *why* it was there, if it was all completely innocent.

'Wait here,' said Holly. 'I'll just go and see if that man has got Chris's address.'

Tracy and Belinda waited by the gate as Holly ran back through the grass.

She was gone only a minute. She came running towards them, holding a small piece of paper in her hand.

'Got it,' she said. 'He's got lodgings in a place called Bewley Street.'

'I know it,' said Belinda. 'Come on, I'll show you.'

They climbed over the gate and went to pick up their bicycles.

'Tracy?' said Holly, giving her friend a hard look. 'You won't say anything stupid to Chris, will you?'

Tracy's eyebrows shot up. 'Me? Like what?'

'Like going up to him,' said Belinda with a knowing grin, 'and saying something like "Is your girlfriend a crook?"'

'Please!' said Tracy, climbing on to her bike. 'Credit me with a bit of intelligence.'

'I do,' said Belinda with a laugh. 'But only a very *little* bit.'

Tracy gave her a look of affronted dignity. 'I won't say a word,' she said. 'I won't even open my mouth.'

Holly smiled. 'This I've got to see,' she said. 'Tracy Foster with nothing to say. Now *that* would be something to put in the school magazine.'

Bewley Street lay over on the north side of Willow Dale. One of the older parts of the town, its old stone buildings had been converted into houses and shops, although there was still some evidence of its previous life as storehouses used in the wool trade.

'I thought that address rang a bell,' said Belinda, bringing her bike to a halt. She pointed over to a shop. Earthenware pots and garden ornaments were displayed out on the pavement, and the windows were filled with attractive pottery jugs and other kitchenware, finished in warm browns and creams. 'This is where my mum buys all the posh flowerpots for her indoor plants,' said Belinda. 'It's run by a woman called Teresa Russell.'

The doorbell rang cheerily as they went into the warm, clay-smelling shop. A small, wiry-haired woman in overalls came out of a back room, wiping her hands on a cloth. Through the back entrance they could see the workshop with a potter's wheel and shelves stacked with unfinished pieces of pottery.

'Can I help you?' asked Mrs Russell, wiping a smear of clay off her cheek. 'You're Mrs Hayes' girl, aren't you?'

'That's right,' said Belinda. 'We haven't actually come here to buy anything, I'm afraid. We were told you had a student staying with you. Christopher Lambert?'

'Oh, you're friends with Chris, are you?' said Mrs Russell. 'He's in his room at the top of the stairs. Go through the back and turn left. You're lucky though, he's just off to visit his folks for a day or two. You only just caught him.'

Belinda thanked her and the three girls went through the workshop and up a narrow flight of stairs.

Belinda knocked on the door.

78

'Just a minute,' came Chris's voice. 'Is that the taxi? I'm almost ready.' He opened the door and stared at the three girls with a smile of surprise.

'We heard about the break-in,' said Holly. 'Are you all right?'

Chris's smile faded. 'Don't talk about it,' he said. 'I feel bad enough about it already. I shouldn't have left the place unguarded, even for a short while. But how did you know where to find me?'

'The man there told us,' said Holly. 'You don't mind us coming over, do you?'

'Not at all,' said Chris. 'It's nice of you to be worried. But I'm perfectly all right.' He smiled again. 'It's not all bad,' he said. 'Anne said there won't be any more work done until Monday now. So I'm taking the opportunity to go over to York to visit my parents. The taxi to the station should be here any minute.'

'Oh,' said Holly. 'That's a pity.'

'Why?' asked Chris. 'What's the problem?'

'No problem,' said Holly. 'I'd hoped you might be able to give me a bit more background on Professor Fairfax for my article in the school magazine, that's all.' Now that it came to it, Holly found herself unable to think of a way of asking about the statue without it sounding like an accusation.

'What did you want to know?' asked Chris. 'You could always ask her direct. I'm sure she wouldn't mind.'

'We didn't want to bother her,' said Belinda.

'We were just wondering about . . . well, about that statue.'

Chris smiled. 'It was a wonderful find, wasn't it?' he said. 'The people at the university are going to be falling over themselves to give her the funds for France now.'

'Yes, I suppose so,' Holly said cautiously. 'But, you see, the thing is— ' She was interrupted by Mrs Russell's voice coming up the stairs.

'Chris! The taxi's here!'

Chris gave them a rueful smile. 'Sorry,' he said. 'I've got to go.' He went back into his room and swung his rucksack up on to his shoulder. 'We can chat some more when I get back, if you like,' he said. 'Or, like I said, you could always talk to her yourselves. She's very approachable.'

But Holly hardly heard what he said. She hadn't noticed the rucksack lying on the floor. It wasn't until Chris picked it up that she even gave it a glance.

But now her eyes were fixed on it, her brain whirling. It was a red and white rucksack. The same red and white rucksack that she had tripped over in the caravan. The rucksack out of which had fallen the mysterious golden statue!

6 Suspicions of conspiracy

'Holly? Are you feeling OK?' asked Chris, noticing the startled look that had swept across her face.

Holly tore her eyes from the rucksack.

She made a feeble attempt at a smile. 'Yes, I'm fine,' she said. 'I – I've been thinking of buying myself a rucksack,' she stammered. 'One like yours. Where did you get it?'

Chris smiled. 'I don't remember. I've had it for ages,' he said. 'There's nothing special about it. You can get them anywhere.' He looked round at the others. 'Look, I'm sorry, but I've got to go. Will you be coming over to Hob's Mound on Monday?'

'Try and stop us,' said Tracy.

Chris headed down the stairs. Behind his back, Holly made frantic gestures at the rucksack bouncing from his shoulder, catching the eyes of her puzzled friends.

'That's the one,' she mouthed at Tracy and Belinda.

'What?' Belinda mouthed back.

'The *rucksack*!' mouthed Holly, jabbing her finger down towards it, her eyes wide.

81

Tracy's mouth opened in a silent, 'Ohhh!' as she understood.

They followed Chris down the stairs.

'That golden statue was *some* find, wasn't it,' said Tracy. 'I'll bet you've never seen anything like it before, huh, Chris?'

At the foot of the stairs, Chris turned with a wide smile. 'Never,' he said. 'It's the sort of thing you dream about.'

Tracy pretended to look surprised. 'Haven't you seen the one in the museum here? It's a lot like the one you found, isn't it?'

A look of unease flicked across Chris's face. 'It's *similar*,' he said. Belinda and Holly glanced at each other. Tracy had promised to keep quiet. What was she going to say next?

'*Identical*, I'd have said,' continued Tracy. 'Almost like a copy.'

Chris's mouth hardened. 'What's that supposed to mean?'

Tracy flashed one of her attractive, innocent smiles.

'Nothing at all,' she said brightly. 'Why? What did you *think* I meant? There aren't any copies anywhere, are there?'

Chris gave her a hard look. 'It isn't a fake,' he said. 'Anyone who thinks Anne is lying about that find is going to look pretty stupid,' he said.

'You mean John Mallory?' said Holly.

'Yes,' said Chris darkly. 'Him, and anyone else.

That statue is the real thing, and anyone who says different is going to have to eat their words once it's been properly authenticated by the university.' He glared angrily at them. 'I've got a taxi waiting,' he said.

Silently, the three girls followed him out into the street. He got into the taxi without speaking again and it drove away.

'I thought you weren't going to say a word,' Belinda said to Tracy.

'I had to say *something*,' said Tracy. 'Neither of you was about to get anything out of him.' She looked at Holly. 'You're sure it was the same rucksack?'

'Oh, yes,' Holly said firmly. 'It was the same one all right. I think we'd better go somewhere where we can have a proper talk about all this.'

Their bikes lay in the grass. The three girls sat themselves under a rugged, old oak tree. The threatening clouds still hung over the distant roof-tops of Willow Dale and overnight rain had been forecast.

'OK,' said Belinda. 'Mystery Club meeting convened. Who wants to speak first?'

Holly opened their red notebook. 'First of all,' she said, 'who believes me now about the statue being a fake?'

Tracy's hand went up. Holly and Tracy looked at Belinda, whose hands had remained clasped in her lap.

83

'Come on, Belinda,' said Holly. 'Look at the evidence. It's obvious. The only thing I got wrong was that I thought the rucksack belonged to Professor Fairfax. Everything else still fits.'

'Except that it was Chris who planted it, and not Professor Fairfax,' added Tracy. 'He admitted he was there that night. It must have been him I saw. And he tried to scare me off with those noises. The only thing we can't know for sure is whether Professor Fairfax knows about it.'

'I'm not saying there isn't something fishy about all this,' Belinda said adamantly. 'And I'm not saying the statue they were showing off yesterday wasn't planted there on purpose by someone.'

'So what are you saying?' asked Holly.

'What facts have we got?' said Belinda. 'One, Holly saw a golden statue hidden in Chris's rucksack.' She counted on her fingers as she spoke. 'Two, Chris just said there were no copies. But, if Holly is right, he had one in his rucksack at the site.'

'What do you mean, *if* I'm right?' Holly said, affronted.

'Don't interrupt,' said Belinda. 'I'm thinking.' She carried on, extending another finger. 'Three,' she said, 'we know Professor Fairfax needed to find something important in order to make sure she got the funds she wanted for this French expedition.'

'Four,' Tracy broke in, 'Chris and Professor Fairfax are having a secret relationship, which is why he planted that copy of the statue from the museum for her to find. He did it to help her get the money from the university.' She looked eagerly at her two friends. 'So she'd be sure of finding something.'

'I was coming to that,' said Belinda. 'The point that you two seem to be missing is that Professor Fairfax has taken the statue off to the university to check that it's the real thing. If it's a fake, how long do you think it would take them to find out? About ten seconds, I should think.'

'I don't know about that,' said Holly. 'It fooled Mallory.'

'Exactly,' said Belinda. 'Do you really think Chris could knock up something *that* convincing? Don't forget, it didn't only have to look right, it had to *feel* like it was made of gold. It had to be as heavy as gold. And it had to pass whatever tests they were going to do on it at the university.'

Holly shook her head. 'You've lost me now,' she said. 'What are you getting at?'

Belinda laughed. 'It's simple,' she said. 'Don't you remember that woman at the museum telling us that all the Celtic stuff was locked away because some students were doing research on it? If my guess is right, we'd find out if we went there that Chris Lambert was one of those students.'

'Oh!' breathed Holly. 'I *see*. You think he stole the real statue. Hid it in his rucksack, and then buried it at Hob's Mound.'

'Elementary, my dear Holly,' said Belinda with a grin. 'The statue that Professor Fairfax has taken off to the university is a real one.'

'Wrong!' chimed Tracy. 'Wrong, because that woman at the museum said she'd *seen* it there. *After* Holly saw the one in Chris's rucksack.'

'That's the really clever bit,' said Belinda. 'If I'm right, the one at the museum is the copy. Chris could have made it out of clay from Mrs Russell's workshop. All he'd have to do is paint it gold. No one's going to double-check on a statue that's already in a museum. It's the perfect crime. Or it would have been if Holly hadn't seen it *before* it was supposed to have been dug up.'

It took a few moments for Belinda's theory to sink in.

'Do you think Chris set this up on his own?' puzzled Holly. 'Or do you think Professor Fairfax was in on it as well? After all, if they're secretly seeing each other, *she* could have arranged the whole thing. She could be using him. You know, *pretending* to care about him, but all the while just using him to get the money she wants for this French dig?'

'That's possible,' said Belinda. 'But before we worry about that, I think we should go over to the museum and check whether Chris *was* one of the students researching the Celtic stuff. We can decide what to do next once we know the answer to that.'

Holly nodded. 'Agreed,' she said. 'Let's go there *now*!'

'Hello,' said Holly, smiling at the woman behind the desk in the entrance lobby of the Willow Dale Museum. 'Remember us?'

The woman nodded. 'Of course. The girls writing the article? I'm afraid the artefacts you wanted to see are still out of circulation.'

Tracy edged forwards, using her most ingratiating smile. 'I guess you couldn't let us have just a quick peek at them, could you?'

'I'd like to help,' said the woman. 'But there's really nothing I can do. The curator has the keys to the back room, and he won't be back until closing time. You could try again later, if you like?'

Holly nodded. 'Perhaps we'll do that,' she said. 'Oh, by the way, you don't happen to know the names of the students who were looking at the Celtic things, do you?'

'Yes, I think so,' said the woman. She opened a drawer and flicked through some papers. 'We had to give them all special passes,' she said, smiling up at Holly. 'You can't let just anyone fool around with these things. Ah, here we are. There were five of them. Mark Boston, Ruth Underwood, John French, Christopher Lambert, and June— '

'Thanks,' interrupted Holly. 'Thanks very much.' She turned to Tracy and Belinda with a triumphant look on her face.

'Come back later,' called the woman as the three girls ran down the steps and out onto the pavement.

'Got him!' said Belinda. 'Ha! I knew I was right.'

'Shouldn't we tell her that we think she's got a fake back there?' said Tracy. 'Someone's got to be told.'

'That's right,' said Holly. '*Someone* has to be told. But if we tell the museum people they'll just call the police, and the whole thing will blow up in Chris's face.'

'So?' said Belinda. 'Why shouldn't it, if he stole the statue?'

'But what if I'm right about Professor Fairfax *using* him?' said Holly. 'Chris would get all the blame, and she'd get away with it. I don't want that to happen if I can help it.'

'What's the plan, then?' asked Belinda. 'We can't confront Chris with what we know. He's gone to York.'

'No, but we can talk to Professor Fairfax,' said Holly. 'Tell her what we've found out.'

'Hang on,' said Tracy. 'Is that such a good idea?'

'It's the only thing we can do,' said Holly. 'We tell Professor Fairfax that we know about her and Chris, and that we're going to inform the police about the statues being switched. If she realises we're on to her, perhaps she'll admit everything. Otherwise, it's going to look as if it was all Chris's doing.'

'And if she *hasn't* got anything to do with it?' said Belinda.

Holly shook her head. 'I don't believe Chris would have done this all on his own,' she said. 'I'm *sure* Professor Fairfax is involved.'

'So how do we get to see Professor Fairfax?' said Tracy. 'If we're intending to confront her with all this?'

'We could try at the university,' said Holly.

'It's thirty-five kilometres away,' said Belinda. 'If you think I'm cycling all the way over there and back, you can think again.'

'I meant we could try *phoning*,' said Holly. 'It should be easy enough to get the number. We phone up, ask to speak to Professor Fairfax, and tell her what we know.'

'And if she isn't there?' asked Belinda.

'Then I ask for her home phone number,' said Holly.

'And if they won't give it to you?' added Belinda.

'For heaven's sake!' said Holly. 'Will you stop inventing difficulties? If we can't get through to Professor Fairfax at all, then we'll just have to come back here later this afternoon and talk to the curator. Tell him all about it. Satisfied?'

'Even if it lands Chris in trouble?' said Belinda.

'Yes,' Holly said in exasperation. 'If we've got no other choice. But let's try getting through to Professor Fairfax first, shall we?'

'No need to get annoyed,' said Belinda with a

shrug. 'I was only trying to be helpful.' She looked at Holly. 'Shall we find a phone, then?'

Holly put the receiver back on to its cradle and stepped out of the telephone booth.

'Well?' asked Tracy impatiently. 'What happened?'

'She wasn't there,' said Holly. 'The person at the other end said I'd missed her by about two minutes.' She glared at Belinda. 'We'd have caught her if you hadn't wasted so much time arguing about it.'

'That's right,' Belinda said drily, 'blame me. Did you get her private telephone number?'

'No,' said Holly. 'They said they couldn't give out information like that. But listen to this. I told them I was writing an article about the dig at Hob's Mound, and I asked them whether they knew if the statue she'd found there had been authenticated yet. They said it had been through all the usual tests, and that it was ninety per cent certain that it was a genuine Celtic relic.'

'Told you so,' said Belinda. 'Didn't I tell you?'

'Will you let me finish?' said Holly. 'They said it was ninety per cent certain, but that Professor Fairfax had decided to consult another expert to make absolutely sure. *That* was where she'd gone. So I asked who the other expert was. You're not going to believe what they said. They told me she was taking the statue over to Professor Rothwell.'

90

'You're kidding!' exclaimed Tracy.

Holly shook her head. 'That's what they told me,' she said. 'I could hardly believe it myself.'

'Well, he *is* supposed to be an expert on that sort of stuff,' said Belinda. 'Even if he is mad as a hatter these days.' She paused, thinking. 'Listen,' she said, 'if she's only just left, it's going to take her at least half an hour to get to the Mad Professor's place. If we go *now*, we might be able to get there first. We could talk to her there.'

'We can wait outside the mill for her to arrive,' said Holly. 'And even if she beats us to it, we can wait for her to come out again. It's the best chance we've got of talking to her. What do you say?'

'Let's do it,' Tracy said determinedly.

They ran to their bikes.

Tracy took the lead, threading her way through the streets of the town and out into the open countryside, her two friends following close behind.

It wasn't long before they were speeding along the narrow country road with fields on either side.

Beyond the bushes, they saw the long back of Hob's Mound. Holly stood on her pedals, looking over the gate as they flashed past. There was no one there. The delve in the barrow's flank was covered by a tarpaulin.

They rode on, leaving Hob's Mound behind them as they covered the mile or so of road that would take them to Professor Rothwell's home. They rounded a curve in the road and Tracy had to swerve to avoid a car that sped towards them. A silver estate car.

It passed her at speed and vanished around the bend.

Tracy jammed on her brakes, the others almost piling into her.

'That was John Mallory!' she shouted back to them. 'Did you see?'

'He was in a hurry,' said Holly, looking over her shoulder. 'He could cause an accident, driving like that.'

'How far to the mill?' Tracy asked Belinda.

'We're almost there,' said Belinda. 'A couple of hundred metres at most. It's just after this bend.'

Tracy pushed off again and the three girls swooped round the long downhill curve. Tall trees leaned over the road, plunging them into a sudden gloom of half-light.

At the bottom of the dip Tracy saw a break in the trees over to the right. A slender track led off the road and into the woodland.

'That's it!' shouted Belinda. 'That's the way to the Black Mill.'

They all spotted it at the same time. The back end of a Land-rover, parked a little way into the track.

They brought their bikes to a halt.

Everything was silent.

'It looks like she got here first,' said Tracy.

Holly frowned. Wheeling her bike alongside

the car, she noticed that the driver's door was slightly ajar.

'That's odd,' she said. 'Why hasn't she closed the door?'

There was no sign of Professor Fairfax. Holly assumed that she must already have made her way up to the Black Mill.

Belinda leaned her bike against the back of the car and walked round, intending to close the car door.

She gave a yelp of fright that brought her two friends running round to her in concern.

A figure lay crumpled face down in the grass. Terribly still.

Holly's hands came up to her mouth in shock.

'Professor Fairfax!' she cried, staring down at the unmoving body. 'It's Professor Fairfax!'

7 The mad professor

The three girls stared in silent horror at the immobile form of Anne Fairfax.

'She's not . . .' Belinda's voice trailed off. She couldn't bring herself to give voice to what she feared.

Tracy knelt and shook Anne Fairfax's shoulder.

'Oh, lord,' she whispered. 'There's blood in her hair.'

'She must have hit her head getting out of the car,' said Holly.

Tracy looked up at her. 'The *back* of her head?' she said. 'No way.' She slid her fingers down on to Anne Fairfax's neck, feeling for a pulse. She gave a low whistle of relief. 'It's OK,' she said. 'She's alive.' She leaned closer. 'Professor?' she said. 'Professor? Can you hear me?'

There was no response.

Tracy looked up at the others. 'Get to a phone,' she said. 'Call an ambulance. I'll stay with her.'

'There's a row of cottages about a mile further on from here,' said Belinda. 'We can try there.'

'Wait,' said Holly. 'What about up at the mill? Professor Rothwell's place? Won't he have a phone?'

'I don't know,' said Belinda.

'You guys go and find out,' ordered Tracy. 'I'll try and make her as comfortable as possible.' She levered the unconcious woman on to her side, putting her in the first aid 'coma' position. She brought her ear close to Anne Fairfax's mouth.

'She's breathing OK,' said Tracy. 'Will you two get out of here?'

Holly ran for her bike.

'It's OK,' shouted Belinda. 'It's not that far.' Giving a final glance at Anne Fairfax's white face, she turned and ran up the gravel slope beneath the overhanging canopy of trees.

Holly hesitated for a moment, then followed her.

'Get the police as well,' Tracy yelled after them.

'Will do,' Holly called back.

She quickly caught up with Belinda. The track snaked round to avoid a steep rise and they came running down and out of the trees. The Black Mill stood stark and solitary ahead of them, a heavy, gaunt building with darkened windows, its crumbling walls knee-deep in wild grasses and tangled bushes, its sloping roof green with moss.

They ran down to the front door. There was no bell. Holly lifted the black iron knocker and brought it hammering down. The knocker was in the shape of an evil face with staring eyes and a wide, leering mouth through which the tongue protruded.

'I don't think this is such a good idea,' Belinda said unhappily as the dull sound of the knocker echoed through the ancient building. 'Do you really think he'd be the type to have a phone?'

'We've got to try,' said Holly. She hammered the ugly face down again, three more times, then listened intently for any answering sound from within. 'Perhaps there's a back entrance,' she said, running along to the side of the mill.

'Holly!' cried Belinda. 'Don't! We'll try somewhere else.'

But Holly was already round the corner, pushing her way through the tangled grasses. A half-ruined wall stretched ahead of her. There was a doorway, but the door lay half-devoured by the encroaching undergrowth of grass and brambles.

The noise and sight of the River Skelter met her. Deep, narrow and fast moving, its brown waters churned and eddied around the lichen-green paddles of a huge, still water-wheel that clung to the back of the mill. Once, the mill wheel would have spun in the rapid waters of the stream, working the machinery that turned the stones to grind the grain. But it looked to Holly as if the wheel had not moved for years.

A little way along the river, a rusty iron bridge spanned the banks, small, narrow and dangerous-looking. It looked as if it might break away from its moorings at any moment and be swept under the dark, flowing water.

'Holly?' Belinda had picked her way round to the back of the mill, her jeans snatched at by spiteful thorns.

'Look!' Holly cried. A small door stood open at the back of the mill, reached by a thin path at the water's edge.

Holly ran along to the door and called. 'Professor Rothwell? Hello? Is there anyone there?'

She felt Belinda's fingers on her arm. 'Holly? Let's get out of here. There's no one home.'

'Let's make sure,' said Holly, stepping over the threshold. 'Hello?' she called.

It was a warm, muggy day, but the old mill was icy cold. It was as if the heat was unable to penetrate the thick stone walls.

They came into a room that was obviously used as a kitchen. It was like stepping back in time. Like entering one of those houses set up to show how people lived in the early years of the twentieth century. Except that there were things on the shelves and on the table that showed more modern habitation.

They walked into a dark hallway. The ivory-coloured walls bulged threateningly towards them as their feet echoed on the threadbare carpet.

There was another open door.

It was a small sitting-room with dark, wood furniture and an old leather sofa. The walls were lined with books and there were more books and papers scattered about. But it was the ornaments and wall-hangings that caught the attention of the two girls. Barbarous masks stared at them. Stone animals and rough, heavy statues roosted in shadows. Celtic faces frowned in the musty silence. Massive black beams sagged above their heads.

'Let's get out of here,' whispered Belinda.

'No. Look!' An old fashioned Bakelite telephone sat on a table by the wall.

'We can't just use it,' said Belinda. 'He might come back any second.'

'This is an emergency,' said Holly, lifting the heavy receiver. 'He'll understand.'

'Will he?' murmured Belinda, looking round at the unfriendly faces that glowered at them.

Holly dialled, giving brief details of the trouble to the ambulance service before being passed on to the police.

She was as relieved as Belinda to put the receiver back and head out into the welcoming warmth of the outside world.

They ran back up and over the rise, praying that Anne Fairfax was safe in Tracy's hands.

Things had changed for the better while they had been gone.

Anne Fairfax was sitting up against the car, her head between her knees, holding a wodge of tissues to the back of her head. Tracy was kneeling beside her.

'Did you get the ambulance?' asked Tracy.

'Yes,' said Holly. 'It won't be long.' She looked at the injured woman. 'What happened?'

Anne Fairfax lifted her dazed face. 'I don't know,' she said. 'Something hit me from behind as I was getting into the car.'

'Mallory!' exclaimed Belinda.

Anne Fairfax winced as she turned her head to look up at Belinda. 'What did you say?'

'We saw John Mallory driving away from here,' said Holly. 'Just a few minutes ago. Was he here?'

Anne Fairfax shook her head slowly. 'I don't know,' she said. 'I didn't see or hear anything.' She took a deep breath. 'I came back from Professor Rothwell. I was just getting into the car when I was hit.'

'You *saw* Professor Rothwell?' said Holly.

'Yes. Down at the mill. I wanted to show him the statue. There was something I needed to check with him. Something strange . . .' Her voice trailed off. 'The statue!' she said with sudden animation. 'Where's the statue? It was in my briefcase.'

They scoured the grass. Belinda looked into the front of the Land-rover. The briefcase was nowhere to be found. The statue was gone.

'You realise what this means?' said Holly. 'John Mallory must have hit you and stolen it.'

'And we saw him escaping,' said Tracy. 'We can tell the police.'

Belinda looked at her watch. 'If they ever get here,' she said.

But was only a few minutes before the police arrived, followed closely by the ambulance.

Anne Fairfax and the girls told the police officers everything they knew about the incident, including the speeding car that had passed them back on the road with John Mallory at the wheel.

'This statue you mentioned,' said one of the officers. 'It's definitely missing? And it's valuable, you say?'

Anne Fairfax looked round as she was being led to the ambulance with a blanket around her shoulders. 'It's priceless,' she said.

The police officer shook his head. 'I don't want to rub it in, Professor, but you don't seem to have much idea of security with these things. First of all you get burglars breaking into your office on the site, and now—'

'Sergeant! Look at this!' One of the policemen had climbed into the Land-rover to make certain that the missing briefcase hadn't fallen inside. He was leaning over the front seats. He unlocked the back door from inside and pushed it open.

The three girls crowded round to look. Lying on the floor of the car behind the driver's seat was a heap of stones and scraps of pottery tied into plastic bags.

'It's the stuff from the caravan!' gasped Holly, recognising the pile of bags.

Anne Fairfax's face whitened. 'I don't understand,' she said. She looked at the suspicious faces of the policemen. 'Honestly,' she said. 'You must believe me. I didn't know they were there.'

'Am I to believe that these are the objects reported stolen from the caravan at Hob's Mound?' said the sergeant, staring at Anne Fairfax.

'Y– yes,' she stammered. 'But I don't know how they got in my car.'

The sergeant's face became stern. 'I think we need to have a little chat, don't you, Professor?'

Holly gaped at the bundle of bags stuffed down between the seats of the Land-rover. There was no doubt in her mind that they were the same bags that she had taken into the caravan a few days ago. But how on earth had they turned up hidden in the back of Anne Fairfax's Land-rover?

Holly's bedroom window overlooked the back garden. The kitchen was full of bulb and flower catalogues, but as yet the garden still had the weedy, neglected look of being fairly low on the list of house improvements. The only sign of activity was Jamie's hole. It had grown somewhat in the past couple of hours, from a shallow trench down at the end to a series of pits and earthworks that resembled a battlefield after a heavy day of shelling.

From her vantage point on the bed, where she was sitting with her two friends, Holly could see the upper half of her brother, digging away with a spade.

'Holly?' said Belinda. 'Are you listening to me?'

'Yes,' said Holly, looking round at her. 'You said you reckon Anne Fairfax staged the robbery herself.' She shook her head. 'I don't see how you make that out, unless she bashed herself on the back of the head.'

'You *aren't* listening,' said Belinda. 'I didn't mean *that* robbery. I meant the robbery from the caravan. *She* broke in there and swiped those bags. So she could sell the stuff off. Don't you remember her telling us that private collectors would pay plenty of money to get them? I'm telling you, Anne Fairfax is behind it all. She's so dead set on getting the money together for that dig in France, that she's prepared to do anything. She got Chris to steal the statue from the museum, as well. It's obvious.'

'I'm glad you agree with me on *that* at last,' said Holly. 'I've been saying Professor Fairfax was behind it all along. But that still doesn't explain us finding her in a heap over at the mill. And it *doesn't* explain us seeing John Mallory driving away from the scene at top speed.'

'Unless she arranged to meet Mallory there,' said Tracy.

'What?' said Holly. 'You mean she *arranged* to be knocked unconcious?'

'Why not?' said Tracy. 'She'd have to show signs of a fight. If you ask me, she set the whole deal up with Mallory. She'd secretly hand over the statue to him. He'd sell it privately, and she'd get the money.'

'Oh, yes?' said Belinda. 'So why didn't he take the other stuff as well? If they're in it together, why leave incriminating evidence in the back of her car?'

Tracy glowered at her. 'Holly's right about you,' she said. 'You're always inventing difficulties.'

'Not inventing them,' said Belinda. 'Just pointing them out. If Professor Fairfax had set up a deal with Mallory, why would he have made that scene at the dig yesterday? It's much more likely that Mallory was watching her, waiting for a chance to get the statue off her. And he got the perfect chance when she took it over to show the Mad Professor. Mallory creeps up behind her, bops her over the head, and makes off with the statue. It's just his bad luck that we came along in time to see him driving away.' She gave her friends a satisfied smile. 'The police will sort him out, no problems. But that still leaves us as the only ones who know what's really been going on behind everything. We've still got to decide what we're going to do about Chris and Anne Fairfax.'

'Tell the police?' said Tracy.

'No,' said Holly. 'Not until we're certain that the statue in the museum is the fake. That will be the final bit of the jigsaw.'

Belinda looked at her watch. 'The museum will

be closing in about half an hour,' she said. 'Which means the curator should be back there soon. And he'll be able to open that back room and check.'

'To the museum, then!' said Tracy.

As they ran down the stairs, they heard Jamie come crashing in through the kitchen, yelling at the top of his voice.

'Coins!' he shouted, waving his fist. 'I've found some old coins!'

He came to a skidding halt, staring at the three girls as they stood laughing on the stairs.

'See?' said Holly to her friends. 'What did I tell you?'

'What are you lot cackling at?' demanded Jamie. 'What's the joke?'

'*You* are,' said Belinda. 'Holly hid those coins there the other day.'

'They're not old coins,' laughed Tracy. 'They're *foreign* coins. What an airhead!'

Jamie stared at the collection of grubby coins in his fist. 'You rat!' he said. 'I suppose you think you're really funny, don't you?'

'I would, if I had time to think about it,' said Holly. 'But right now, we're in a hurry.'

'I'll get you for this, Holly Adams,' shouted Jamie as the three girls headed for the front door.

Holly glanced over her shoulder. 'If I were you, I'd be more concerned about what Mum and Dad are going to say about the state you've got the garden into.' Mr and Mrs Adams had gone off for the day. They were unlikely to be impressed by Jamie's efforts in their absence.

'Yah! Get lost!' shouted Jamie as the girls jumped on to their bikes. 'I wasn't fooled by those coins anyway. I was just pretending!'

'Dream on!' Holly called back, as they sped along the road towards the museum. 'Dream on, Jamie!'

'You realise this can't help but get Chris into trouble?' said Belinda as the three girls mounted the steps to the museum entrance.

'I know,' Holly said unhappily. 'But maybe when they realise that it was really Anne Fairfax at the bottom of it, they won't be too hard on him.'

An unexpected scene met their eyes inside the museum.

The woman from the reception desk, and another man the girls didn't know, were trying to quieten Professor Rothwell. The old man was standing in the middle of the first exhibit room, shouting and waving a thick walking-stick.

'Professor Rothwell!' gasped Holly. 'What's he doing here?'

'Going crazy, by the look of it,' said Tracy.

They ran into the room. The strange man, who the girls took to be the curator, was vainly trying to catch the old man's arm. He jumped back as the stick whirled.

'Professor, please,' he shouted. 'Calm yourself!'

'I demand to see the Elfbolt Hill artefacts!'

shouted the old professor, his hair flying, his wrinkled face red with wrath. 'You have no right to hide them from me!'

'We haven't hidden them,' exclaimed the curator. 'I *will* show them to you, if you will only give me a moment.' He ducked as the stick whipped through the air.

'Thieves!' shouted the old man. 'Thieves and rascals.'

'Phone the police,' the curator called to the woman.

Belinda stepped forward, hoping she might be able to say something to calm the old man. After all, he did seem to think there was something special about her.

'Professor?' she said. The old man spun at the sound of her voice. His stick accidentally hit the front of the empty Celtic remains display cabinet.

There was a terrific crash and a shriek of an electronic alarm. Belinda threw her arms up to protect herself as splinters of broken glass came hurtling towards her.

8 Ride into danger

The flying fragments of glass from the shattered display case sent everyone diving for cover. There was a peal of glass on the tiled floor as the sound of the alarm rang in their ears.

Belinda's eyes had closed instinctively, and when she opened them again, it was to see Professor Rothwell hunched over, one hand cradling his wrist, a look of pain on his face. His walking-stick lay on the floor.

'Great heavens!' gasped the curator, almost speechless as he stared from the broken case front to the old man.

Holly ran forward, a protective arm coming round Belinda's shoulders.

'Are you all right?' she asked.

Belinda nodded. 'I think the professor is hurt,' she said. She stepped towards the old man. 'Professor? Have you been cut?'

'My wrist,' mumbled the old man. The accident seemed to have drained him of anger.

'Mrs Cruickshank.' The curator looked over to the woman. 'Switch the alarm off. And fetch the

107

first-aid box. Quickly, please.'

Tracy ran to get a chair. The professor sat down. All thought of calling the police was forgotten as they gathered around the old man.

It was only a small wound, a nick at the side of his wrist. As they tended to the old professor, his pale eyes turned to the curator. The shrill alarm stopped abruptly.

'Where are the Elfbolt Hill artefacts?' The old man's voice was quiet. 'You have no right to keep them from me.'

'They aren't being *kept* from you, sir,' said the curator.

'Then why have you taken them from their cabinet?' asked the professor.

'Students have been using them for research papers,' explained the curator. 'They're in the work room.'

'Get them,' said the professor. 'If you're telling the truth, show them to me.'

The curator looked uneasily at him. 'I shall,' he said hesitantly. 'If you give me your word that you will remain calm. Your word, sir.'

The professor nodded. 'I am perfectly calm, Mr Webber.'

'Very well,' said the curator. He looked at the girls. 'Will one of you help me, please?'

Holly followed him.

'Are you going to call the police?' she asked, as they walked through the museum.

'I'd very much rather not,' said Mr Webber. 'Professor Rothwell was a great man in his time.' He glanced round at her. 'He had a nervous breakdown, you know. I don't believe he has ever really recovered from that.'

'He does seem very confused,' said Holly. She explained their previous encounters with the old man.

The curator nodded sadly. 'I know that he's become eccentric,' he said. 'I only hope I'm doing the right thing by letting him see the pieces from Elfbolt Hill. He found them, you know.'

'Yes,' said Holly. 'I know. Did he say why he wanted to see them?'

'Apparently the statue they found at Hob's Mound is similar to the one he dug up at Elfbolt Hill. Professor Fairfax took it to show him.' The curator shook his head. 'She shouldn't have done that. It stirred up old memories for him. It's very sad.'

This didn't seem the right moment to say anything about the Mystery Club's suspicions. Not while Professor Rothwell was at the museum.

'I'm hoping that once he's seen them, we'll be able to convince him to go home,' said the curator. 'I don't want to have to call the police. The damage he's caused isn't serious. There's no need for other people to be involved.' He took a bunch of keys out of his pocket as they approached a closed door.

The room beyond the door had the look of a

laboratory. There were long work benches supplied with equipment for weighing and measuring, as well as a bank of electronic equipment and a computer terminal. On one bench stood two wooden boxes, like drawers from a cabinet. Placed carefully in the boxes were the finds from Elfbolt Hill. Statues and brooches and carved stones. Lying on a bed of tissue, Holly saw the golden statue.

The curator paused. 'I hope I'm doing the right thing,' he said.

'I'm sure you are,' said Holly. She smiled hopefully. 'Perhaps once he *sees* these things, he'll realise that he's been . . . mistaken. You know, about the legends, and everything. At least I hope so.'

They lifted the boxes and carried them out.

Tracy had found a broom and was sweeping the shards of glass together. The professor, a bandage tied round his wrist, was standing quietly to one side.

His eyes became strangely bright as he saw Holly and the curator approaching. He stumbled forwards.

'Give them to me,' he cried. 'I must take them back. They belong in the earth.'

'Professor!' The curator stepped back with renewed alarm, trying to keep the box out of the old man's reach. 'You gave me your word!'

'Fool!' shouted the professor. 'These things don't belong to you! I'm going to take them back to the

110

grave mound where they were found.'

His fingers snatched for the box, knocking it out of the curator's hands. There was a crash as the box tipped and its precious contents of brooches and ornaments fell to the floor, the golden statue amongst them.

'Professor Rothwell!' shouted Belinda, dashing in front of him. 'Please, you don't know what you're doing.'

He stared into her face.

'He will come for you,' the professor said, his voice trembling. 'He will drag you down into the darkness.' His eyes blazed round at the others. 'Fools!' he said. He turned and strode towards the entrance. 'I've done all I can,' they heard him shout. 'On your own heads be it.'

Belinda let out a long breath as the old man vanished down the steps and was gone.

'Crazy,' breathed Tracy.

But something else had caught Holly's attention. She crouched, picking up the golden statue from where it had fallen.

'Look,' she said softly. 'Look!' The head of the statue was broken off. The break showed brown. She looked at Belinda. 'You were *right*,' she said. 'It's pottery. It's the *fake*!'

The curator listened in stunned silence as the three girls told him about Anne Fairfax and all that they had found out and guessed about the faking of the discovery at Hob's Mound. The evidence of the broken statue was too compelling for him to disbelieve them.

He gave the keys to Mrs Cruickshank. 'Lock up for me,' he said. 'And don't touch anything. I'm taking these girls to the police station.'

Leaving their bikes chained up outside the museum, the girls got into Mr Webber's car. As they drove, Holly couldn't help feeling a twinge of regret that it would be their evidence that would condemn Chris Lambert. Especially as she was now convinced that it was Anne Fairfax who was at the bottom of things.

A further surprise was to confront them as they made their way into the police station. John Mallory was there, at the door. He gave them a withering glance as he pushed past them, his fingers buttoning his jacket.

Something about his hands puzzled Holly for a second, but she had no time to think about it, as he forced his way between them and strode along the pavement.

'They've let him go,' whispered Tracy. 'I can't *believe* they've let him go.'

There was no time to discuss it as Mr Webber led them into the police station.

They only had to wait for a short while before being shown into an austere side room. Two police officers took notes as the three girls gave their statements. Knowing glances passed between the two officers as Holly told them about seeing the statue in the caravan.

'You've been very helpful,' said one of the officers. He smiled at Holly. 'You're very sharp-eyed,' he said. 'We could do with more like you around.'

'But what about the *real* statue?' blurted Tracy. 'Haven't you charged that Mallory guy with stealing it?'

The police officer shook his head. 'Mr Mallory has been questioned and released without charge,' he said. He stood up, smiling again. 'You can go now,' he said. 'Don't worry, you'll be hearing from us in due course.'

'I don't get it,' said Tracy as they came out on to the pavement. 'We *saw* that Mallory guy driving away from the scene of the crime. How come they let him go?'

'I'm sure the police know what they're doing,' said Mr Webber.

'I'm sure they do,' said Belinda. 'I just wish *I* knew what they were doing.'

Mr Webber drove them back to the museum to pick up their bicycles.

Cycling home, Holly felt a depressing sense of anticlimax. Now that their findings had been passed to the police, there was nothing more for the Mystery Club to do. It seemed terribly unsatisfying, the idea of sitting around waiting to hear what happened next. But what other choice was there?

Now that the police were involved, it didn't seem that there was any further role for Holly and her friends to play.

It seemed that the mystery of the golden statue was over.

It was early Sunday morning. It had rained heavily overnight, but the clouds had finally been blown away to leave the sky a bright, rain-washed blue. Holly was kneeling on her bed, her elbows on the windowsill, looking out of the window. At the bottom of the garden she could see Jamie diligently digging away. She was surprised that nothing had been said about the mess he was causing. Especially now that his holes were a mire of mud. She assumed that, it being the weekend, her father hadn't been out to his workshop, and that neither of her parents had taken a recent look out of the back windows. She was pretty sure that there would be plenty of trouble when they did.

Holly had shrugged off the gloom of the previous evening. She still felt bad that Chris was in trouble, but there was nothing she could do about it now, and, as Belinda had pointed out, he *had* stolen the golden statue, whatever his motives had been. There was no getting away from that.

But there was still something irritatingly *unresolved* about the mystery. Like an itch she couldn't quite scratch. Some little thing that was lurking in the deep recesses of her mind.

She heard the telephone and scrambled off her bed to go and answer it.

It was Kurt.

'Have you heard?' he said breathlessly. 'They've picked up Anne Fairfax. The police, I mean. My dad's just heard from the newsdesk.'

One good thing about Kurt was that, having a father who ran a newspaper, he always seemed to know what was going on in Willow Dale before anyone else. 'Apparently she's confessed to having stolen that golden statue from the museum,' he continued. 'You know, the one she pretended to have found. And she's admitted to taking the stuff from the caravan. Although she's still insisting she was hit from behind, and that the statue was taken from her. Isn't it incredible?'

'I know most of that,' said Holly. 'I think it was *us* that put them on to her.' She explained the Mystery Club's visit to the police station. 'But I didn't expect her to confess to taking the statue from the museum. We didn't think that was her. We thought it was Chris. Do you know if Chris was mentioned at all?'

'Yes,' said Kurt. 'He was, as a matter of fact. Professor Fairfax said he had nothing to do with it. She's told the police that he knew nothing about it at all.'

'Well, I'm glad about that, at least,' said Holly. 'I always sort of hoped he wasn't involved.'

'You're a lot of rats, though,' said Kurt with a

laugh. 'Why didn't you let me in on all of this? What a scoop!'

'We weren't sure,' said Holly. 'Not until Professor Rothwell broke the fake statue. But we thought John Mallory had taken the real statue. We saw him driving away from there.'

'Yes,' said Kurt. 'I heard about that as well. Apparently the police picked him up within minutes of Anne Fairfax being attacked. He hadn't even left his car. The statue wasn't on him, so they had to let him go. They didn't think he could have had time to hide it anywhere.'

'Oh,' said Holly. 'That explains it.'

'There's something else,' said Kurt. 'The police officers who touched those bags of stuff they found in Anne Fairfax's car have come up in this really bad rash. No one can figure out what it is.'

Holly's mouth dropped open. 'The itching powder!' she said. 'I can't have wiped it all off.'

'What did you say?' asked Kurt.

'Itching powder,' explained Holly. 'It's a long story, but I spilled some itching powder over the bags, and . . .' Her voice faded, her eyes widening as something snapped into focus in her mind. 'Kurt? Listen, I've got to go. I've just realised something. I'll phone you later.' She slammed the receiver down before Kurt had time to reply.

Belinda had got the itching powder on her and had come up in a rash. And now Holly realised what it was that had puzzled her about John

Mallory's hands as he had buttoned his jacket on leaving the police station the previous afternoon. His hands had been covered in red weals. Exactly the same kind of marks that Belinda had shown her.

A rash caused by itching powder. He *must* have touched those bags. There was no other explanation.

Holly wracked her brains. Had Anne Fairfax been suffering from the same rash when she had seen her yesterday morning at the Black Mill? She tried to picture the scene again in her mind. Anne Fairfax holding a clump of tissues to her injured head. But had there been a rash on her hand?

No! Holly felt sure about this, as sure as she could be under the circumstances. Anne Fairfax's hands had been normal coloured. Which meant she *couldn't* have touched those bags.

Which also meant she couldn't have been the person who stole the bags out of the caravan, despite her confession. Someone else must have done it. And that someone else would have the rash. And the only other person Holly had seen with a rash on his hands was John Mallory.

What's going on? thought Holly. *Is Professor Fairfax protecting John Mallory? But* why *should she do that? It doesn't make sense.*

Her heart racing in her chest, Holly dialled Belinda's number. She let it ring unanswered for half a minute before she gave up and rang Tracy.

'We've got to tell the police,' cried Tracy as the importance of Holly's discovery hit her. 'Have you spoken with Belinda?'

'I couldn't get a reply,' said Holly. 'Look, I'll cycle straight over to her place. Meet me there. She's probably out with Meltdown. As soon as she gets back we'll all go straight to the police.'

Holly's legs pumped up and down on the pedals as she sped towards Belinda's house. She was thinking hard.

Surely Anne Fairfax hadn't confessed to the theft of the bags from the caravan to protect John Mallory? Why should she do such a thing? Holly couldn't make sense of it.

But Holly did know one thing no one else could possibly know. She knew about the itching powder. She *knew* Mallory was involved with the burglary – and she could prove it.

And once the Mystery Club had passed this information to the police, surely it would be only a matter of time before they worked out that it was Mallory who had hit Anne Fairfax and stolen the statue.

And then, thought Holly, *perhaps we'll find out what is really behind all this, and why Anne Fairfax has confessed to something she didn't do.*

Belinda patted Meltdown's glossy neck.

'Good boy,' she panted. '*Good* boy. That was fun, wasn't it?'

She loved these long Sunday morning rides over the wild Yorkshire hills. Just her and Meltdown, and no one else for miles. The rain clouds were gone and the sun was shining on her back. The turf was springy beneath the horse's thudding hooves.

She had urged Meltdown up a long ridge, giving him his head as the wind whipped at her hair and pinched her cheeks until they were red.

It wasn't until she reined him in and caught her breath that she realised where their gallop had taken them.

Below her, in the flat fields over to her left, she saw the thrusting back of Hob's Mound. And beyond the open fields was the screen of woodland that hid the River Skelter and the Mad Professor's Black Mill.

Almost without conscious thought, her fingers came up to touch the dobbie stone that she still wore around her neck. It felt cold. Almost as cold as the inside of that strange old house where the peculiar old man lived.

She slapped Meltdown's neck. 'At least it's not raining any more,' she said. 'It really poured down last night, didn't it, boy?'

A sudden thought struck her. When Chris had taken them to the Bloody Well earlier that week, he'd told them that the stream ran red after heavy rain.

'I wonder if it rained heavily enough last night,'

murmured Belinda. 'Shall we go and see, boy? Shall we go and see if that stream is running red like Chris said it would? I've never seen a red river before.'

She gazed at the woods. 'Except that I don't really want to go too near the Black Mill,' she said. She thought for a moment, then nudged Meltdown forwards with sudden resolve.

'We don't believe in Professor Rothwell's spooks, do we, boy?' she said. 'Of course we don't. So let's go and take a look at that well. And if it's as interesting as Chris said, we can come back here and show Holly and Tracy later, can't we?'

Meltdown walked towards the huddle of dark trees.

'We're not frightened by that old man, are we, boy?' said Belinda. 'There's nothing to be frightened of at all.'

It was easy enough to be rational on the sunlit uplands, but, as Meltdown picked his way carefully in amongst the trees and the twilight gloom of the overhanging branches engulfed her, Belinda felt a pang of unease.

Perhaps this hadn't been such a brilliant idea after all. To get to the Bloody Well, she would have to pass quite near the Black Mill.

She leaned low over Meltdown's neck, the branches snatching at her hair like grasping fingers.

There was something a bit eerie about this

particular stretch of woodland. A feeling of being watched. Of something lurking just out of sight.

And it didn't help that she seemed very quickly to lose her bearings.

'Look at that,' she said, speaking aloud to break the ominous silence. They had come to an area where the land crumpled itself into folds and dips, like an unmade bed. Ahead of them she saw a black mouth in the rising hillside. A cave mouth, half hidden by bracken.

'Chris told us about all these caves,' she said, guiding Meltdown to the left, hoping that the low crease they were heading down would lead her back into more familiar territory.

With a suddenness that tore a scream from her throat, something dark came bursting out of the shadows, rising up almost under Meltdown's hooves.

The horse reared, whinnying, and Belinda felt herself falling backwards, the reins slipping out of her fingers and the tangled canopy of leaves wheeling across her eyes as she was hurled towards the ground.

9   Prisoner!

Holly brought her bike to a stop in the broad gravel driveway of the Hayes's luxurious hilltop house. Mrs Hayes was out in the front, half hidden by a huge rose-bush. Holly could hear the neat snick of pruning scissors.

'Hello!' called Holly, wheeling her bike over.

'Good morning, Holly.' Mrs Hayes was dressed in immaculate gardening clothes, her perfectly groomed hair protected by a headscarf, her feet clad in green wellingtons. Mrs Hayes was a woman who had a complete set of clothes for every occasion. 'Aren't the roses looking lovely? Mr Connor does a marvellous job with the garden,' she confided. 'But I do like to get out here when I can.'

'Is Belinda home?' asked Holly, after making some polite comments about the roses.

'She's out riding,' said Mrs Hayes. She looked at her watch. 'She's been gone a good while now. She shouldn't be long.'

Holly heard wheels crunching on the gravel. It was Tracy arriving on her bike.

'Why don't the two of you wait for Belinda down

at the stables?' suggested Mrs Hayes. 'She should be back any time now.'

The two girls walked their bikes down the long garden path, resting them against the stable wall.

'Trust Belinda to be missing when we need her,' said Tracy.

'A few minutes won't make any difference,' said Holly. 'And she'd throw a fit if we went to the police without her.'

They skirted the buildings at the bottom of the Hayes's long garden and hung over the fence. A narrow bridle-path wound its way down the hill and off out into open countryside.

'I still think there's something screwy about Anne Fairfax's confessions,' said Tracy. 'OK, so *she* did the switch at the museum – not Chris – I can follow that. But she sure didn't steal that stuff from the caravan. We know that was Mallory.'

'Perhaps she got Mallory to do it for her?' suggested Holly. 'If the stuff was stolen, it could be sold off quietly without any suspicion falling on her. Perhaps she's been secretly working with Mallory all along.'

'So why did he hit her and make off with the statue?' said Tracy.

'Maybe he got greedy,' said Holly. 'Maybe he decided he wanted *all* the money from selling the statue, rather than just taking a cut and giving the rest to her. I'm just glad that her confession has proved Chris wasn't involved after all.' She

123

smiled at Tracy. 'It would have been terrible for him if Anne Fairfax *hadn't* confessed, wouldn't it? All the evidence we'd collected about the faking of the statue pointed straight at him.'

'True,' said Tracy. 'Including the fact that you saw the statue in his rucksack. I guess she must have hidden it in there without him knowing, huh?'

'I suppose so,' said Holly. She peered down the long, winding path. 'Come on, Belinda,' she said. 'Where *are* you?'

Belinda lay gasping on the ground, winded by her fall. Her glasses had been shaken loose and she seemed to hurt everywhere, but her instinct was to pick herself up and catch hold of Meltdown's reins before he bolted. She sat up with a groan. It was too late. The frightened horse was already galloping back through the trees.

Someone loomed over her, blotting out the dappled sunlight and, before she had time to react, she felt hands helping her to her feet.

'Are you all right?' asked a familiar voice.

She blinked short-sightedly and Professor Rothwell's face swam into focus. 'That was a nasty fall. I didn't mean to startle you. Are you hurt?' he asked.

'N – no,' stammered Belinda. 'I don't think so.' Belinda was more angry than anything else. 'What were you playing at?' she demanded, pulling herself together after the shock. 'Springing out like that? I could have broken my neck.' She looked for Meltdown, but he was already out of sight.

'*Brilliant!*' she exclaimed. 'Now look what you've done. He's probably halfway home by now. Where are my glasses?'

Professor Rothwell stooped and picked up Belinda's spectacles. She put them on, relieved to find them intact.

The old man caught hold of her wrist. 'I only meant to warn you,' he said, staring intently at her, his voice taking on the urgent, insistent tone that she had heard before. 'I knew you would come, Epona. I knew you would be drawn here. You don't realise your danger. The grave is open now. There's nothing to stop Cernunnos from taking his revenge.'

Belinda listened to this mad tirade as unease tingled up through her anger.

'I wasn't *drawn* here,' she said. 'Let go of me.' She tried to pull her arm away, but the professor's grip was surprisingly fierce.

'Listen, Professor,' she said calmly, supressing her rising dismay. 'Let me go, please. I'm not this Epona you keep talking about. My name is Belinda. Belinda Hayes. I – I don't understand *any* of this. It's all . . . listen, *please* listen to me – all this stuff about goddesses and magic, it's all just *legends*. It's not true, none of it. Can't you see that? I'm just an ordinary girl.'

The old man's grip relaxed, but the wildness was still in his eyes.

Belinda attempted to smile. 'I've got to catch my horse,' she said. 'My mother will be frantic if he turns up at home without me.'

'Yes,' murmured the old man, releasing her wrist. 'Yes, I see.' He rubbed his hand across his eyes. 'You're name's Belinda?'

'That's right,' said Belinda.

The old professor gave her a puzzled look. 'Have I been mistaken?' he mumbled, hardly seeming to be speaking to her at all. 'Have I misunderstood things?'

'I think so,' said Belinda with a reassuring smile. 'I . . . I think you've got a bit confused, that's all.'

'Confused?' said the professor. 'Yes. Yes, that's it. I was . . . confused.' His voice suddenly strengthened. 'How will you catch your horse?'

'I don't know,' admitted Belinda. 'Don't worry, though. He knows his way home. I'll just have to follow him.' She sighed. 'It's a bit of a hike.'

'Your mother will be worried, you say, if he gets back without you?' asked the professor. 'Would it be better if you were to telephone her? To let her know you're safe? I have a telephone.'

'No, that's all right,' said Belinda, reluctant to go back to the Black Mill.

'You don't want your mother to worry,' said the

old man. 'Come along, it's the least I can do. It was my fault you fell in the first place. Telephone your mother and then I can drive you home. There's no sense you walking all that way.'

Belinda looked dubiously at him. 'I suppose not,' she said. 'But I shan't need a lift. My mother will come and pick me up.' She nodded. 'OK,' she said. 'I'll use your phone.'

The old man seemed normal enough now as they walked down through the trees towards the Black Mill.

Perhaps he really does believe me, now, thought Belinda. *Perhaps he really has snapped out of it*.

The cold atmosphere of the Black Mill raised goose-bumps on her arms. The professor led her in through the back way, through the old kitchen and into the hall. She was about to mention her previous visit here, with Holly, and that they had used his phone, when he gave her a sudden push.

She stumbled through a doorway and heard the door crash shut at her back. She spun round, hammering on the door with her fists.

'Professor!' she shouted. 'Let me out!'

'You must stay here,' came his voice through the heavy wooden door. 'You must stay here until the danger is past. He is *calling* to you, Epona. The horned god, Cernunnos, is drawing you towards him. I will protect you. Don't be afraid, I will protect you.'

Belinda beat her hands on the door. 'Professor!'

But there was no sound from outside. With a groan of despair, Belinda turned and leaned against the door, sliding down to sit hopelessly on the floor.

'You might be protecting me from this horned god of yours,' she groaned. 'But who on earth is going to protect me from *you*?'

'Look at the time,' said Tracy. 'I thought her mom said she'd be back any minute?'

The two friends had been hanging about now for half an hour, waiting for Belinda to come back. Holly had gone into the stables and had fetched a pair of binoculars that were kept there in the tack room. She was perched on top of the fence, scanning the rolling downs for a first sight of Belinda's return.

'How typical,' continued Tracy, warming to her theme. 'She's never around when there's anything important to be done. Holly, are you listening to me?'

'No, not really,' said Holly distractedly. She could see something small and dark away to the west, but it was too far off for her to be sure. It had emerged from the shade of the trees. She stood up precariously on the fence, turning the wheel on the binoculars to try and get a better focus.

'Oh!' Her gasp of surprise brought Tracy climbing up beside her.

'What is it?' asked Tracy. 'Let me look. Is it Belinda?'

'No,' said Holly. 'It's Meltdown. I'd swear it was. But there's no one on him. Take a look yourself.'

It took Tracy a few moments to bring the binoculars to bear on the small dark, trotting shape away over near the deep green of the distant woodland.

'You're right,' she said. 'It's *him*, OK. Oh, no. You don't think she's had a fall, do you?'

'I don't know,' said Holly. She jumped down off the fence. 'Do you think we'll be able to ride our bikes over there? It's pretty rough ground, but it's too far to run.'

'Shouldn't we go up to the house and tell her mom?' said Tracy.

'What could she do?' said Holly. 'You couldn't drive a car over there, and she'd only go into a panic. No, let's find out what's happened first. One of us can always shoot back here if it's something serious.'

It wasn't too bad down the bridle path, but once the two girls were in the open countryside, their bikes rattled and shook alarmingly, the wheels skidding on hummocks as they forged their way towards the place where they had seen Belinda's horse.

The rise and fall of the hills blocked their view and it was a couple of anxious minutes before they caught sight of Meltdown again, trotting towards them with his reins dangling.

'Should I catch him?' suggested Tracy.

'No, leave him,' said Holly. 'He'll find his own way back. We've got to find Belinda.'

Meltdown had come out of the trees, and it was into the trees that the two girls headed, steering their bikes over the smoothest ground and calling out Belinda's name.

It became impossible to keep their bikes upright. They left them leaning against a tree, and raced deeper into the woodland, shouting at the tops of their voices.

It was a desperate business. The woods *seemed* to be full of tracks and pathways, but every line they took eventually petered out into nothing.

'What was she *doing* in here?' panted Tracy. 'What kind of idiot tries to ride through *this*?'

'I don't know,' gasped Holly. 'Perhaps she saw something. Perhaps she was following someone? How should I know what she was – oh!' The trees came to an abrupt halt and the two girls found themselves staring out across the sleek brown waters of the River Skelter.

'That does it,' said Tracy. 'We've come the wrong way. We'll have to go back.'

'No, wait. Look!' Holly pointed. A few hundred metres downstream the trees drew away from the river, leaving a small clearing. In the middle of the clearing, backing on to the river, they saw the gaunt stone walls and the immobile wooden wheel of the Black Mill.

'That's Professor Rothwell's place,' said Holly. 'I hadn't realised we'd come this far.'

'So that's where the Mad Professor lives?' said Tracy. 'What a creepy-looking place. It's no surprise he's half off his head.'

'I wonder,' breathed Holly. 'You don't suppose Belinda came this way, do you? I mean, what if she caught sight of Professor Rothwell and followed him? That would explain her coming into the woods.'

'Why should she follow him?' asked Tracy.

'You said yourself that no one would want to ride through here,' said Holly. 'And you're right. No one would. Unless they had some reason.' She pointed to the grim building. '*That* might be the reason. I think we should go and check it out. Unless you've got any better ideas.'

Tracy shook her head, and followed Holly's lead towards the lonely mill.

As they approached the mill, they came to a startled halt.

Through the rampant undergrowth they saw the shape of a car parked at the front of the building. Not Professor Rothwell's car. A silver estate car. Neither of them needed to speak; they both recognised it immediately.

It was John Mallory's car.

And while they were still taking this in, they heard a noise. A huge creaking, grinding, churning noise that came from the back of the mill.

131

'What's that?' hissed Holly, looking round at Tracy. 'What on earth is that?'

Belinda could almost have laughed. Whatever the professor was, he certainly wasn't a very efficient jailer.

The room he had locked her in was bare floored, the few items of heavy furniture thick with dust. Light filtered in through a small, murky, cob-webbed window. It was locked, but as far as Belinda could see, it was her best means of escape.

She picked herself up and hunted for some-thing either to break the narrow pane of glass or to chisel her way through the frail-looking lock.

It was behind an old wardrobe that she discov-ered the thing that brought a grim smile to her face. Half hidden and obviously forgotten by the professor, was a low doorway.

She put her back to the wardrobe, bracing her feet and heaving with all her strength. Wood screeched on wood as the wardrobe inched away from the wall.

Belinda squeezed herself into the grimy space. There was no handle on the door, but there was no lock either. She slid her finger into the hole where the handle had once been and jerked the door open.

Dust cascaded over her. She pushed through the narrow gap and found herself in a dim, enclosed wooden stairwell, like the kind that wind up inside a castle turret. Disturbed dust filtered down and spiders' webs fluttered around her as she crept up the creaking treads.

She came to a low, square exit. Crouching, she found herself in a room filled with immense old wooden machinery. She was on a kind of landing, or gallery. It was a wooden platform high above the large stone mill room. Through the slatted outer wall she could see segments of the mill wheel, and beneath her, still in place, were the great grinding stones that had once turned wheat into flour.

Her only problem was that there seemed no way down from there. A ladder lay away down on the floor, uselessly out of reach. Even looking down there made her feel giddy.

A hollow, echoey booming sounded from somewhere down in the building. It sounded different from inside than it had from the outside, but she recognised it. It was the sound of the ugly old door knocker rapping on the mill's black front door.

Her heart gave a leap. The professor had a visitor. Whoever it was, they couldn't be as crazy as him, she thought. All she needed to do was yell and she'd be rescued.

Distorted voices came to her ears. Angry voices. The professor's voice and another, much louder. A man's voice. Shouting.

Belinda frowned. She knew that other voice. She'd heard it somewhere before, recently.

The voices came closer and she drew in a sharp breath of recognition. It was John Mallory. She was *sure* of it.

Any lingering doubts were swept away as a door down at ground level flew open and the old professor came lurching into the room beneath her.

Belinda ducked in amongst the bulky wooden mill machinery, lifting her eyes over a huge cogwheel. John Mallory stood in the doorway.

'You old fool,' he said. 'I didn't come here to listen to your gibberish. I want to know what you've done with the statue.'

'It must go back into the earth where it was found,' said the professor. 'The horned god is awake.' He pointed a shaking finger at John Mallory. 'His power is growing. No one will be safe.'

Belinda saw John Mallory's eyes narrow. 'You're mad,' he said. 'You've lived with this nonsense so long that you can't even tell what's real any more.' He stepped into the room. 'It was you, wasn't it? You knocked that Fairfax woman out, didn't you? You hit her and took the statue, you old fool.' He gave a hiss of anger. 'I wish I'd realised it at the time. To think I was so *close* to it then and didn't know it. If only I'd waited until she came back to the car.' He advanced into the room. 'You don't understand a thing I'm talking about, do you?' said Mallory. 'You don't know night from day, any more.'

Belinda saw the professor back away. 'I know you're working with the horned god,' gasped the old man. 'I can see the evil in your face.'

Mallory laughed harshly. 'There is no horned god, you fool. I'm working for myself. I wish I'd known she had that statue on her when I followed her here yesterday. You would never have got your hands on it. *I'd* have taken it. Sold it, and retired on the money. There'd have been no need to try and discredit her, then. I wouldn't have needed to try and frame her with the things from the robbery. It wouldn't have mattered *who* was running the dig, if I'd been able to get my hands on that statue.' He pounced forwards. 'Where have you put the statue?' he shouted, grabbing the old man's shoulder. 'Where have you hidden it?'

'I'll tell you,' gasped the professor, writhing in Mallory's vicious grasp. 'I took it up to the cave. But you mustn't go there. It must be returned to the Mound. You don't see the danger we're all in.' His voice rose to a shriek. 'The horned god!'

'What cave?' John Mallory's eyes blazed. 'Blast you and your fairy stories! What cave are you talking about?'

'It's up . . . up in the woods,' cried the professor. Belinda saw him give a sudden twist of his shoulders, tearing himself out of John Mallory's grip.

Mallory was after him in a second. The old man stumbled. His hands flailed, catching a long wooden lever as he fought for balance. With a protesting creak of ancient wood, the lever came thudding downwards under the old man's weight.

Belinda leaned over the cog-wheel. The professor was sprawling on his back, Mallory crouched over him, looking as if he was about to hit the defenceless old man. Belinda couldn't let that happen. Whatever happened to her afterwards, she couldn't stand by and see the old man hurt.

Immense grindings and groanings of slowly moving wood filled her ears. The machinery of the mill was beginning to turn! Belinda shrank back, her heart thudding, her head spinning with the noise that surrounded her.

She saw the light flickering behind her. She turned in terror. All around her the cog-wheels and spindles were in motion as the huge mill wheel started to rotate. With a shock of pure panic she realised that the lever the old man had fallen on must have been a locking device for the mill wheel. His fall had released it.

As she tried to get away from the grinding machinery, she felt a sudden tugging at her sweat-shirt. She tried to pull herself free, staring down in horror to see the hungry teeth of the cog-wheel churning. The waist of her sweatshirt was caught between the cogs.

Her feet slid on the floor and she let out a piercing scream as the machinery slowly drew her closer and closer into its crushing embrace.

10   Escape into darkness

'What's Mallory doing *here*?' said Tracy as the two girls stared through the overgrown brambles at the silver estate car parked at the front of the Black Mill. 'Do you think he's some kind of *friend* of the Mad Professor?'

'I suppose he could be,' Holly said uncertainly. 'Except that Professor Rothwell didn't strike me as the sort of person who *has* friends.' She glanced towards the river. 'Keep an eye on the car,' she told Tracy. 'I'm just going to see if I can find out what that noise is.'

Holly ran to the side of the mill. The source of the noise was revealed immediately. Spumes of white water cascaded from the lifting paddles of the huge old wheel as the fast flowing waters of the River Skelter beat against it.

But the question that filled her mind was *why* the water wheel should have started up. As she had noticed before, it looked as if it hadn't been in use for decades.

She saw a narrow window, deep set in the thick stonework. The sight that met her eyes through the window sent her stomach tumbling.

She stared through into the mill room, its grey walls sweeping upwards to a high roof. Professor Rothwell was lying on his back near the millstones, and crouched over him was John Mallory, his arm raised as if to rain blows down on the old man.

Almost without a pause for thought, Holly snatched up a large stone that lay by the wall and hurled it at the glass.

As the glass shattered she heard a scream. But it wasn't from either of the two men. It was the high-pitched scream of a girl.

Mallory's head snapped round as Holly's stone bounced across the floor in a peal of splintered glass. He was on his feet in an instant, alert as a cornered rat. After a moment's hesitation, his face contorted with shock, he was running for the open door of the mill room.

Holly heard a second scream. It came from high up inside the room. She picked up another stone and began hammering away the shards of glass that still clung to the narrow frame.

Professor Rothwell was sitting up, his hands to his face. As Holly brought her knee up on to the sloping stone sill, she saw the professor stagger to his feet, his face turned upwards. He was bent over, grasping a wooden lever in both hands and pulling upwards.

Holly flung herself through the window, landing on all fours.

'Help me!' shouted the professor, heaving at the lever. 'Your friend's been caught in the machinery.'

'Holly!'

Holly stared up at the frantic sound of Belinda's voice. There, on a high platform, Holly could see Belinda struggling hopelessly to free herself as the gnashing cog-wheels dragged her ever closer.

She was only seconds away from being crushed between the wheels. There was no time for questions. Holly scrambled up and brought her own strength to bear on the lever. It rose slowly in a deafening tumult of screeching wood.

In the sudden silence Holly heard Belinda's voice from above her head, yelling in incoherent relief.

'The ladder!' shouted the professor. 'Help me get the ladder up to her.'

'Belinda? Are you OK?' Holly called up. Over the edge of the high platform she could see Belinda's white face staring down at her.

'Get me out of here!' Belinda shouted down, her voice trembling. 'This thing's trying to eat me!'

'Are you hurt?' Holly called.

'No. But I can't move,' called Belinda. 'It's got my sweat-shirt.'

It wasn't easy, getting the heavy old ladder upright, but between them Holly and the professor managed to balance it on its end and tilt it so that it came thudding against the lip of the lofty platform.

Professor Rothwell held the ladder as Holly climbed.

Belinda was pinned up against two enormous cog-wheels, her ruined sweat-shirt caught in the teeth.

Holly stared at her.

Belinda shook her head. 'Don't ask,' she said. 'Just get me out of this.'

'Is she safe?' called Professor Rothwell.

'Yes,' Holly shouted down. 'More or less.'

Between them, the two girls managed to prise Belinda's sweatshirt loose. It had suffered badly in the cog-wheels.

'You're lucky it's so baggy,' said Holly. She grinned in relief. 'It'll be baggier than ever now.'

'No jokes, please,' said Belinda with a wavering smile. 'That was a bit too close for comfort. It almost made mincemeat of me. What are you doing here?'

'I was going to ask you the same question,' said Holly. She quickly explained how they had seen Meltdown and had ended up at the Black Mill.

'But what on earth made *you* come here?' asked Holly.

Belinda stepped to the edge of the platform, clinging on to Holly for support. 'He did!' she said, pointing down at the professor. 'He conned me into coming here, then locked me up.' Belinda looked round at Holly, lowering her voice. 'He's really not with it, Holly,' she murmured. 'He's still going on about those legends. He really believes it, you know. I mean, *really* believes it.'

They heard the sound of rapidly approaching footsteps, and Tracy came hurtling into the room.

She skidded to a halt. 'Professor Rothwell,' she gasped. 'I'm sorry, your front door was open, and I – I thought my friend had . . .' Her voice trailed off.

'Up here!' called Holly.

Tracy stared up at her. 'That Mallory guy!' she shouted. 'I just saw him. He's gone. What are you doing up there?'

'Coming down,' said Belinda. Holly held on to her as she gingerly stepped down on to the ladder. 'I *hate* heights,' hissed Belinda as she cautiously felt her way down to ground level.

Holly climbed down behind her.

Belinda stared at the professor. 'You nearly got me killed, I hope you realise that!' she exclaimed.

'I'm so sorry,' mumbled the professor, his hand to his head. He swayed and the three girls ran forwards to help him.

'Come on, Professor,' said Holly. 'Let's get you to a seat.'

Without protest the professor allowed them to help him into his sitting-room. He crumpled into an armchair. He looked exhausted and frail. He stared up at them with puzzled eyes.

'What have I done?' he quavered. 'What have I been doing?'

'I don't know,' said Holly. 'What *have* you done?'

The old man's head fell against the back of the chair.

'It wasn't Mallory who knocked out Professor Fairfax,' said Belinda, nodding towards the old man. 'It was *him*!'

'So where does Mallory fit in?' asked Tracy. 'He came running out of here like his tail was on fire. I thought he'd – I don't know *what* I thought.'

'He came here to get the statue from Professor Rothwell,' said Belinda. 'I heard it all.' She told her friends everything that had passed between John Mallory and the professor.

A new animation came into the old man's face. 'You must stop him,' he said. 'You mustn't let him get the statue.' He stared at the girls. 'It's all right,' he said. 'I'm all right now. I've been . . . confused.'

'You said that once before,' said Belinda sharply, 'and I ended up locked in that room.'

The professor shook his head. 'No, I understand now. I'm not talking about ghosts. John Mallory is a bad man. He mustn't be allowed to take the statue. We must phone the police. I've got to try and explain.'

'Tracy?' Holly looked at her friend. 'Where did Mallory go? Did you see?'

'That was the weird thing,' said Tracy. 'He didn't head for his car. He came crashing round the side.

He would have run straight into me if I hadn't ducked out of the way. He was heading back the way we came. Into the woods.'

'Towards the cave!' said Belinda. 'He's gone to find the statue. The professor hid it in a cave.' She turned to the old man. 'Is it that cave near where I fell? The one over in the woods?'

'Yes,' said the professor. 'The statue isn't far inside. It's just by the entrance.' He reached out towards Belinda. 'Forgive me for putting you in danger,' he said. 'I wasn't in my right mind.'

Belinda smiled. All the craziness had gone from the old man's face. 'As long as you're OK now,' she said.

'I am,' said the professor. 'I must telephone the police. All this has got to be brought to a stop. That poor woman, Professor Fairfax. I struck her and took the statue. How could I have done such a thing?'

'You phone the police,' said Holly. 'Belinda? Do you think you could find that cave again?'

Belinda nodded eagerly. 'Easily,' she said. 'And we might even be able to get there before Mallory if we're quick. All he knows is that the statue is in a cave in the woods. He doesn't know where the cave is exactly, does he, Professor?'

The professor shook his head, pulling himself up out of the armchair. 'Go,' he said. 'See what you can do. But don't go near Mallory. He's dangerous.'

The three girls ran from the Black Mill, skirting the river, heading for the trees.

They plunged into the woods, Belinda in the lead, three pairs of ears pricked for any sound of the man they knew was also in there, searching for the cave mouth. They passed the place where Holly and Tracy had first come upon the river. Ahead of them the river looped northwards and the land began to rise into tree-covered hills. They pushed onwards through the foliage, leaving the river's edge.

It took Belinda only a few moments to orientate herself.

'This way,' she said, recognising the crease in the landscape down which she had been riding Meltdown when she had encountered Professor Rothwell.

They crept silently forwards, staring through the trees for any sign of John Mallory.

'This is it,' said Belinda, pointing up the slope to where the black cave mouth yawned behind its screen of brambles.

They scrambled up the slope. The cave stretched deep beyond daylight, like an open throat in the hillside.

'We'll never find anything in there without some light,' said Tracy. 'It's pitch-black in there.'

'The bike lamps,' said Holly. 'We could use them. Belinda, you stay here. Keep out of sight and watch for Mallory. Don't let him see you.'

'Don't worry,' said Belinda. 'He won't find me. I've already seen what he's capable of.'

She found herself a hideaway a few metres from the cave mouth, behind a broad swathe of thorny bushes.

Cautiously listening for Mallory's approach, Tracy and Holly picked their way through the trees to where they had put their bikes.

They were on their way back to Belinda with the lamps when Tracy suddenly caught Holly's arm.

'Shh!' she hissed. 'Look!'

A dark shape was floundering through the undergrowth twenty metres or so away. It was Mallory. He was moving away from them and they could hear him cursing.

Holly gave a soft laugh. 'He's completely lost,' she whispered to Tracy. 'Come on. We can find the statue and be back at the professor's place before he gets anywhere near the cave.'

Belinda's head bobbed up from behind the bushes as they approached.

'No sign of him yet,' said Belinda. 'I think we've beaten him.'

'We saw him,' said Tracy. 'I think he's headed in the wrong direction.'

'Let's not waste any time,' Holly said urgently. 'He could be back this way at any minute.'

The mouth of the cave was just over a metre high, the jagged lip of rock petering away to either side in a flattened fan shape.

145

'Oh, well,' said Holly, switching her lamp on. 'Here we go.'

The lamp threw up patterns of light and shade over the low, arched roof of the tunnel.

'I'll stay near the entrance,' said Belinda. 'Someone's got to keep a look out just in case Mallory finds it.'

She watched as her two friends went crouching down the tunnel, their bent shapes black against the light of their bike lamps.

'Can you see anything?' said Tracy, her voice strangely flat, absorbed by the stone that surrounded them.

'There's some kind of opening,' said Holly. The tunnel ended in an arch of blackness, the light stretching out over a flat, sandy floor littered with stones.

They came into a cave, not much bigger than an ordinary room. Boulders stood out starkly in the sudden light, throwing dense black shadows over the walls. At the back of the cave was a dark crack. Another tunnel, thought Holly, straightening her back and sweeping her lamp around the uneven walls of the cave.

'There's Anne Fairfax's briefcase,' said Tracy, her lamp sending its pool of yellowish light on to the discarded case.

They ran over to it. Holly pulled it open. There were papers and documents in it, but no sign of the statue.

146

'What's happened to it?' asked Tracy.

Holly sent her light prowling over the rock-strewn floor.

She gave a cry of delight. 'There!' Something flashed gold. The small statue was lying on a flat-topped rock at the far end of the cave. 'Tracy! We've got it!'

'Great,' said Tracy. 'Let's get out of here.'

Holly picked up the statue. It felt icy cold.

They heard a scrabbling noise behind them. Belinda's face appeared, twisted with concern.

'He's *here*!' she gasped. 'It's my own fault. I just stuck my nose out for a second and he saw me. He's coming. What are we going to do?'

'We can jump him as he comes in,' said Tracy. 'He won't know there's three of us.'

'I wouldn't like to try it,' said Belinda. 'He's really vicious. You didn't see what he was like with the professor.'

Holly spun her light to shine on the crack at the back of the cave. 'Perhaps that leads to somewhere we can hide?' she said.

'That's crazy,' said Tracy. 'He'll follow us.'

'Remember what Chris told us about these caves,' said Belinda. 'He said it was like a maze in here. Maybe we could find some way of hiding and then doubling back on him?'

'I don't know,' said Tracy. 'It sounds kind of risky.'

'Not as risky as standing here waiting for him,'

said Holly. In the quiet that followed this remark, they could all hear the sound of someone entering the mouth of the tunnel.

'Go for it!' said Tracy.

The three girls ran for the black slot in the cave wall. They entered the crack in single file, Holly leading and Belinda at the back. There was no roof to it, just a rapidly diminishing fissure between the rock faces.

Holly led them through a switchback of sudden changes of direction as the tunnel gradually widened on its way deep into the hillside. They came into a cell of stone from which different-sized tunnels led like spokes from the hub of a wheel.

'Now what?' said Belinda.

'Hide,' said Holly, flashing her light towards a low tunnel mouth.

They had to get down on all fours to make their way into the tunnel. They edged themselves away from the entrance.

'Lights off,' said Holly. 'They'll give us away.'

Their breathing sounded magnified out of all proportion in the absolute darkness that enveloped them when they switched off their bike lamps.

They strained their ears for the sound of pursuit.

Belinda was nearest the mouth of the tunnel, and it was she who first saw the light flickering.

She pulled her legs up under her, pushing back against Tracy in an effort to get deeper into cover.

They held their breath.

Through the low arch of the tunnel entrance they could see an unsteady light fill the cave. Not torchlight. A light that wavered like pale flame.

They heard the sound of feet crunching slowly on the cave floor.

This was a terrible idea, thought Holly. *He's bound to find us.*

The light grew stronger. Belinda blinked as a small tongue of white flame danced in front of her eyes.

Beyond the point of fire she saw John Mallory crouching, staring straight at her. He was holding a cigarette lighter in his outstretched hand.

'Ha!' His voice was a harsh rasp. He ducked his head and groped into the tunnel, catching hold of a loose fold of Belinda's sweat-shirt.

She tried to pull away. Tracy and Holly grabbed her arms and dragged her backwards. There was a ripping sound and Mallory's fingers lost their grip as her two friends jerked Belinda deeper into the constricting tunnel.

'Stupid fools,' hissed Mallory. 'You can't get away.'

'Can't we?' shouted Tracy, hoping she sounded braver than she felt. 'Just you watch us!'

'Give me the statue.' Mallory crawled into the tunnel, the lighter illuminating the grey walls.

Belinda kicked out and managed to hit Mallory's fist.

Fathomless blackness engulfed them as the cigarette lighter was knocked out of his hand.

Holly grabbed Tracy's hand, scrambling further along the tunnel, still hoping they could find some way of escaping.

A sudden emptiness opened under her blindly groping hand and she felt the ground slide away from under her.

Holly's heart leaped up into her throat. Her stomach turned over as she fought for balance, feeling herself beginning to slide downwards.

Tracy heard the gasp of Holly's breath. Realising that something was wrong, she grabbed out into the darkness. She caught hold of Holly, but in stretching forwards Tracy brought herself too near the crumbling edge.

As she clung on to Holly, she felt the ground slip away under her knees. The two girls teetered on the precarious edge for an agonising moment before tipping over into the sliding blackness.

With cries of despair, Holly and Tracy tumbled head over heels, down and down the endless black slope, the rush and fury of stones all about them as they fell.

11 Lost in the caves

Belinda curled herself up in the darkness, trying to breathe silently, trying to control her panic.

There was no sound from Holly or Tracy.

She tried to make sense of what had happened. They had been right in front of her. One moment she was bumping against Tracy as the three of them crawled away from John Mallory's groping hands. Then there had been that terrible noise like a rock-fall – a clamour of sliding and bouncing stones, and the screams of her two friends, rapidly shrinking away into deadly silence. And in the silence, Belinda had realised that she was on her own. Tracy and Holly were gone.

Heavy, rasping breath filled the tunnel. Belinda could hear the *pat, pat, pat* of hands searching. John Mallory was feeling through the darkness for his lost cigarette lighter.

Belinda didn't know what to do. She didn't dare move for fear of falling over the same gulf that had claimed her friends. It was like being in a horrible nightmare. A pitch-black nightmare from which there was no waking up.

Behind her the darkness gaped, ready to swallow her, as it had swallowed Holly and Tracy. In front of her Mallory was creeping forwards. If she stayed where she was, it would be only a matter of seconds before Mallory found his lighter and she would be revealed in the flickering flame.

She was paralysed with fear and dread. She tried to gather her scattered thoughts, but the blood pounding in her ears blotted out everything else. Her trembling fingers clenched round the dobbie stone hanging from her neck.

The ancient Celtic stone that was supposed to protect her. To protect her from things like *this*!

Belinda became aware of something painfully hard jutting up into her side. A rock, she thought. Something she could use as a weapon to fend Mallory off. Something she could throw at him to give herself a few seconds to think.

She lifted herself and felt under her. It wasn't a rock. The thing was smooth, with straight edges. It was one of the bike lamps. She closed her hand round it, comforted a little by the feel of a normal, everyday object in this terrifying black world under the hills.

But it wasn't just that thought which lifted Belinda's spirits. A lamp meant light. And light was the one thing she craved more than anything else. She didn't even care about John Mallory at that moment, just as long as she could find out what had happened to her friends. It was all too easy to imagine every sort of horror in this cold, sunless place.

Steeling herself for whatever would come next, she lifted the lamp, angling it down the tunnel, and switched it on.

Mallory gave a cry, flinging his arm up across his face, blinded by the sudden blaze of electric light.

Belinda risked a glance over her shoulder. Now she understood what had happened. She was almost at the end of the tunnel. Behind her the walls opened out into another, much bigger cave. To one side the humped and uneven floor fell away in a long, angled drop, like the downward slope of a roof.

Holly and Tracy must have blundered over the edge. Belinda's heart pounded in her throat. They could be lying injured down there. Or even worse.

She crawled to the edge and shone the lamp down. About four metres beneath her, the roof of the cave pitched low, and the slope swept downwards under it, beyond the reach of her light.

'Holly!' she shouted. 'Tracy?'

A brightness flared a few centimetres down the slope. The golden statue was caught against a corner of rock. Belinda stretched down and retrieved it.

'Holly!' she called.

Belinda thought she heard a faint, answering

153

voice out of the depths. But it could have been just an echo of her own cries.

A much closer sound brought her head snapping round. John Mallory's hand came down on the back of her neck.

'Give me that lamp.' His voice was harsh.

'My friends,' gasped Belinda, wincing under the voice of his fingers. 'They're down there. They might be hurt.'

'Ha!' Mallory's eyes glinted as he caught sight of the statue in Belinda's hand.

'Help me,' Belinda cried in desperation. 'We've got to do something.'

'Give me the statue!' snarled Mallory.

'No!' Belinda flung her arm out over the slope, the statue gleaming in her hand. 'Let go of me, or I'll drop it. I *will*!'

Mallory's hand lifted from her neck, his eyes narrowed with a mixture of greed and uncertainty.

Belinda scrambled away from him on all fours, shining the light into his face.

'You're being stupid,' said Mallory, his hands up to shield his eyes. 'You can't get out without coming past me. Give me the statue and I'll let you go.' His mouth twisted in a cunning grimace of a smile. 'Or do you want your friends to stay down there?'

Belinda stared at him, trying to guess his thoughts. He was right about one thing: there was no way for her to get to the tunnel without him being able to grab her.

'If – if I give it to you . . .' she stammered. 'You'll help me?'

'Of course,' said Mallory, reaching out towards her.

Belinda didn't trust him. But what other option did she have? She glanced again down the slope.

Reluctantly she held the statue out towards his clutching hand.

It seemed to Holly that the fall would never end. The noise of sliding stones was all around her. Tumbling debris, loosened by her fall, struck against her body like hail. At any moment she dreaded that the rock face would dip away under her and she would be hurled into a black gulf.

She came to a thudding halt, the breath driven out of her body by the impact. She lay gasping and dizzy as a flurry of stones bounced over her.

She opened her eyes on to endless nothingness.

A heavy weight pinned her legs. She lifted her bruised arms and felt for what she thought would be a smothering prison of rocks. She felt clothing under her fingers. The weight wasn't rock at all; it was Tracy, sprawled across her legs in the thick, dusty aftermath of their fall.

She heard Tracy cough.

'Tracy?' Holly choked, her lungs clogged with dust.

'Yes,' came a faint reply.

'Are you OK?'

'I think so.' Holly felt Tracy's weight lift from her legs. 'Oh, lord,' gasped Tracy. 'I hurt all over. What happened?'

'The ground just gave way under me,' said Holly. 'How far do you think we've fallen?'

'Who knows!' groaned Tracy. Holly heard the rattle of stones as Tracy struggled to her knees. 'Did you manage to keep hold of the lamp?'

'No. I lost it somewhere,' said Holly, sitting up. 'What about Belinda?'

'She was behind me,' said Tracy. 'I guess she must still be up top.' Her voice was tinged with despair. 'Holly? What are we going to do?'

'Feel around,' said Holly. 'Try to find the lamp. It must be around here somewhere. I had it in my hand when I fell.'

The two girls groped in the dark. It became clear to Holly how they had managed to avoid being seriously hurt. The ground beneath her felt like sand of fine grit, banked up at the foot of the slope. It was hard and dry, but it had cushioned them against injury.

'Got it!' said Tracy after a few moments. She picked the torch up. It felt oddly light. 'Oh, no!' she groaned. 'It's come to bits.' All that she had in her hand was the plastic sheath.

'Keep searching,' said Holly, crawling towards the sound of her friend's voice.

Gradually, piece by piece, they found the batteries and the rest of the lamp. It had only come into three pieces, but it seemed to take a lifetime of trial and error to reassemble them.

'How difficult can it *be*?' said Tracy as she tried over and over again to screw the small bulb into its hole in the concave front of the lamp. 'I mean, it's not like we're trying to build a nuclear power plant down here.'

'Which way in do the batteries go?' asked Holly.

'I don't remember,' said Tracy. 'Just stuff them in anyhow and we'll see what happens.'

A faint cry came filtering down.

'Shh!' said Holly. 'Did you hear that?'

'Belinda!' breathed Tracy.

Holly took a deep breath. 'We're OK!' she shouted.

They listened for a response.

'Ow!' Holly threw her arms over her face as light splashed into her eyes.

'It works!' crowed Tracy. 'Oh, sorry.' She shone the light away from Holly's face. 'We did it, Holly!'

The two girls smiled at each other.

'Gosh,' said Tracy. 'Look at the state of you!'

'And you,' said Holly. Their tangled hair was full of grit and dust and their faces were grimy with dirt. Tracy patted her clothes, sending up clouds of stone dust.

Holly looked around, getting her bearings. They were in a huge, low-ceilinged cavern. Gravelly sand dunes undulated away to distant, invisible walls.

The chute down which they had fallen showed as a dark slot, like an enormous letter-box at the edge of the sunken roof.

Tracy stood up, the roof just brushing her hair. She shone the light up the slope.

'We'll never get back up there,' she said, eyeing the steep rise. 'Not without ropes and stuff.' She looked round at Holly. 'They're bound to go for help, aren't they?' she said. 'I mean, that guy isn't so off-beam that he'd leave us here, is he? Belinda will sort something out with him, huh?'

Holly stared up the slope. The ceiling of rock dipped, blocking off a clear view to the top.

'Shout up to them,' said Holly. 'Both together. We've got to let them know we're OK.'

They stood side by side at the bottom of the hole.

'Ready?' said Holly.

Tracy nodded. 'Ready.'

They filled their lungs with air and let out a shout that went echoing up into the darkness.

Belinda was a split second from surrendering the golden statue when she heard their voices come reverberating up the slide.

The acoustics of the place robbed the double-voiced shout of meaning, but at least she now knew they were alive. And that knowledge gave her a breathing space.

She snatched the statue away from Mallory.

'You're not having it,' she said, keeping the light in his eyes. 'You let me *out* of here.'

Mallory's lips curled in a snarl. Belinda could see by the tension in him that he was preparing to pounce at her.

'I'm warning you,' she said. 'You touch me and you're going to be in worse trouble than you already are.' She was glad that her voice didn't betray her fear. 'Professor Rothwell has already called the police,' she said. 'They'll be here any minute. Even if you get the statue off me, you won't be going anywhere with it.'

Belinda stood up, training the light on him.

Even though she was half-expecting it, Mallory's sudden spring towards her took her off guard. And the look in his eyes suggested that he intended more than just to get the statue from her. He looked as if he was prepared to give her some of what he had intended for the old professor.

With a scream, Belinda turned and fled, running away from the slope over which her friends had fallen, the lamplight skittering over the cave walls as she leaped over the treacherous, uneven floor.

She heard his shout of rage, and then another sound. A heavy, grating thud. She flicked a look over her shoulder. He had tripped over a rock that jutted from the floor. Even as she looked round, he was already getting to his feet, but it had given her a few precious seconds. And by the difficulty he had in getting up, it looked as though Mallory had injured himself.

But it was not enough to stop him. He came limping after her, his face a mask of pain and rage.

Concentrating the light down at her way ahead, Belinda pounded along the rubble-strewn floor of the cave, jumping over obstacles, looking out for some gap in the walls that she could dart down. Chris had said the caverns were like a maze. Perhaps she would still be able to lose Mallory in there without losing herself.

She climbed over a slithery hump of rock and came bumping down into a high, narrow gorge of rearing stone. The way ahead was broken into slabs like giant steps. She jumped down from step to step, not daring to look round, but knowing that Mallory could not be far behind.

A sheer face of stone confronted her. A dead end. But, no! There was a crack in the rock over to her left. A possible escape route.

She squeezed through and came out into a vast empty space. It was a cavern bigger than any she had seen, like a cathedral of stone. But the worst of it was that the ground ended abruptly at her feet. She was on a ledge of rock that led to nothing.

She swung her lamp, desperately seeking some way out of her predicament. Sheer stone walls rose behind her, broken only by the crack she had come through.

The chase was over. All she could do was wait for John Mallory's inevitable approach.

He edged through the crack, panting, his face twisted with the pain of his fall. He was limping heavily and there was a murderous look in his eyes.

He gave a low croak of laughter as he saw that Belinda had no place to run.

She backed away, to the edge of the rock shelf.

Mallory caught her arm, prising her fingers loose from the statue.

'Now!' he whispered, pulling the statue out of her hand. 'Now what do I do with you?'

Belinda ducked sideways. She was desperate. Unless she fought back, there was no knowing what Mallory might do to her.

She felt the dobbie stone hanging heavily against her chest. It was just the thing.

She tore the stone from round her neck and backed away from Mallory, swinging the stone round her head on its leather thong.

'Keep away from me!' she shouted.

Mallory came at her. She spun the stone with all the force she could muster. It cracked against the side of his head and he let out a bellow of pain. He stumbled on to one knee, dropping the statue. It teetered on the lip of rock and Belinda lunged to try and grab it.

She felt the rock crumble under her feet. For a moment she balanced on the edge, her arms windmilling, and then the rock gave way beneath her and she fell.

The fall was thankfully brief, no more than three metres, and her landing was soft and yielding as icy water splashed up over her.

She was on her feet, but ankle-deep in freezing mud. The bike lamp wheeled in her hand, momentarily showing her a moving stream of black water before she overbalanced. The lamp shot out of her hand and blinked out as it vanished into the water.

She pulled her hands out of the clinging mud and dredged her way to firmer ground, feeling in the blackness for a way out of the mire.

The mud sucked at her, but her hands hit solid stone. She pulled herself on to the invisible boulder and lay gasping for breath. She listened for any sound from Mallory, but there was nothing other than the pounding of her own heart and the rush of the underground river.

The relief of having escaped John Mallory's revenge gave way to a realisation of her peril. And the statue was still up there. Mallory had it. Her flight had been a waste of effort, and had left her in worse danger than ever.

She groaned. What she had to do now was find her way to the surface. That was *all*!

Think! she said to herself. *Don't panic. Think*!

A light dawned in her head. The river. This had to be the underground river Chris had told them about. The river that came out at the Bloody Well. It was flowing to her left. If, in all this impenetrable darkness, she could somehow feel her way downstream, then maybe, where the waters rose overground, she would find some way out. Chris had said there was a pothole somewhere near where the river came out. An exit from the caves. If only she could find it. It was her only hope.

Summoning up all her courage, she began the desperate journey to light.

And when I do get out, thought Belinda, *I'm going to have something to say to Holly about the messes she keeps getting me into!*

'Do you think they heard us?' asked Tracy. There had been no answering cry from above. 'You don't think something's happened up there, do you?'

'We've got to get up there somehow,' said Holly. 'Belinda would have called back if she'd heard us. I've got this horrible feeling Mallory might have done something to her. I lost the statue. It must still be up there.' She looked into her friend's anxious face. 'Shine the light around, Tracy,' she said. 'See if we can find some way out of here.'

But the low walls of the cavern were frustratingly solid.

'We can't give up,' said Holly. 'We've got light. We must be able to do something.'

'Let's try this way,' said Tracy, leading off along the wall. 'We're bound to find *some* way out.'

She looked at Holly. 'We'll get out,' she said uncertainly. 'We will, won't we?'

Holly didn't give voice to her thoughts. Chris's words came back to her: you could get lost in those caves for ever. Chris had likened the caves to a maze, but there was one big difference. A maze would eventually let you out. These caves could wind and twist their way for miles, and there was no certainty at all of them ever finding a route to the surface.

But it wasn't in Holly's nature to dwell on such things. They *would* get out. That was what she concentrated her mind on as she followed Tracy. Somehow they *would* get out.

'Can you hear something?' said Tracy. They had travelled about fifty metres through the shifting sand, keeping close to the wall.

They listened.

There was something. A faint, ghostly sound in the endless stillness. Coming from ahead of them.

'It's water,' said Holly.

'Water!' gasped Tracy. 'That's all we need. A quick swim to cheer us up. Too bad I didn't bring my swimsuit.'

'At least it'll be something to drink,' said Holly. 'To clear the dust out of our throats. I'm really parched.'

They scrambled up a high bank of sand that almost touched the roof. Beyond it they saw that the sand gave way to red mud. And threading its way rapidly through the mud banks was a stream of dark water.

But there was more. Something revealed in the oval of light thrown down by their lamp. Something so unexpected that they could hardly believe their eyes.

12 *The Bloody Well*

'Belinda!'

Holly's yell of delight echoed around the huge cavern as she and Tracy slid down the sand bank towards their friend.

'You took your time finding me!' shouted Belinda. 'Careful. Don't get too near the water. The mud's like glue!'

Holly and Tracy quickly realised the truth of what she said as the red mud came sucking up over their shoes. Belinda was ankle-deep in the stuff and it plastered her almost from head to foot.

Screwing her eyes up against the light, Belinda reached out towards them and they pulled her free, supporting her between them as they fought their way back to the dry sand.

Belinda sank down into the sand with a groan.

'Holly?' she said faintly. 'Remember when we set up the Mystery Club?'

'Yes,' said Holly, crouching by her side and trying to scrape some of the mud off Belinda's jeans.

'Remember I asked if it was going to be energetic,

166

and you said all we'd be doing was lying around reading books?'

Holly gave a faint grin. 'Yes, I remember.'

'You never said anything about me almost getting chewed up by old mill gears,' said Belinda, looking at her through mud-spattered glasses. 'You never mentioned that I'd be getting chased through caves by some lunatic after my blood. And you certainly never told me I'd end up frozen half to death and covered in mud.'

'It's not *my* fault,' said Holly. 'I don't plan these things.'

'So whose fault is it?' asked Belinda. 'These things never *used* to happen to me.'

'None of us would be here if you hadn't decided to go nosing around in the Black Mill,' said Tracy.

'Nosing around?' exclaimed Belinda. 'I went there to use the phone. I didn't know I was going to get locked up.'

'Then you've got to be pretty dim, if you ask me,' said Tracy. '*I* wouldn't have gotten caught like that.' She grinned. 'But at least one good thing's come out of all this.'

'Oh, yes?' said Belinda. 'Such as what, exactly?'

Tracy pointed towards Belinda's torn, mud-caked sweat-shirt. 'You'll have to throw that old thing away at last.'

A wide grin spread across Belinda's face. 'Didn't you know?' she said. 'I've got a whole drawer full of them at home.'

Tracy shook her head. 'You're *hopeless*,' she said.

'I don't want to interrupt or anything,' Holly cut in. 'But shouldn't we be thinking of some way out of this mess?' She looked at Belinda. 'What happened up there? We heard you yelling, then it all went quiet. What happened with Mallory?'

Belinda described her ordeal, leading up to her fall into the water and the loss of her lamp.

'You should have seen the look on his face,' said Belinda. 'I really thought he was going to *kill* me to get his hands on that statue.'

'The statue!' said Tracy. 'What happened to it?'

'I don't know,' said Belinda. 'He had hold of it, but he dropped it when I clouted him with the dobbie stone.' She shook her head. 'To be honest with you, I don't much care what happened to it, or him. I just want to get out of here.'

'Can we go back the way you came?' asked Holly.

'I don't think so,' said Belinda. 'I *fell*, remember. And it's all soft mud back there.' She reached up and her friends helped her to her feet. 'I was following the line of the river. Remember Chris showing us where it came out? At the Bloody Well? He said there was a pothole near there. I was hoping that I might find it if I kept near the river.'

'That's assuming it's the same river,' said Tracy, sending the light of her lamp shining out over

168

the dark water. The river was a deep, rusty-red colour.

'It is,' said Belinda. 'It must be. See how red it is? Chris told us that when it rained a lot and the river got higher, it ran red because of the mud. I've been trying to figure out the distances. The cave we came in through can't have been more than a kilometre from the Bloody Well. And we must be between the cave and the well, don't you think?'

'There's one way to find out,' said Holly. 'Tracy, is it my imagination, or is that light fading a bit?'

The pool of lamp light had been white, but now as the three girls looked, they could see that it had turned a much dimmer yellow.

'I wasn't going to mention it,' said Tracy. 'It's your lamp, Holly. When did you put the batteries in?'

'I don't remember,' said Holly. 'Ages ago.'

'Then we'd better get on with it,' said Belinda. 'I've had one lot of trying to find my way in the dark. I don't fancy doing it again.'

There was no option but to follow Belinda's plan. They walked in single file, Tracy lighting their path.

Holly tried to be optimistic, but she couldn't help thinking how easy it must be to lose track of distance and direction in this endless darkness.

Corners and sharp angles of rock began to rise out of the sand. A few more metres and they were climbing over bare rock that glinted in the lamplight. The river narrowed between stony banks and ahead of them they could hear a new sound. The sound of falling water.

A ledge rose in front of them, the river plunging through a dark slot carved in its face.

Belinda sank to her knees. 'I can't,' she said. 'It's no good. I can't climb any more. I'm exhausted. It's *hopeless*.'

'I'm not giving up,' said Tracy. She looked at Holly. 'Give me a leg up. I'll go see what's coming up.'

'More rock,' said Belinda. 'And then *more* rock.'

The ledge was only chest height. Holly boosted Tracy up. As Tracy crawled forwards they watched the patch of lighted rock shrink to a faint glow.

In the darkness, Holly took hold of Belinda's hand.

'We can't give up now,' she said. 'We're almost there.'

'Are we?' came Belinda's tired voice.

'Of course,' said Holly. 'You'll see.' She squeezed Belinda's hand. 'Anyway,' she said. 'I'm not letting you give up. Who's going to look after Meltdown if you don't get out of here?'

It was only a few moments before the light returned and they saw Tracy's face over the lip of rock.

'There's a waterfall,' she said. 'Only a small one. And then a sort of lake. We can get down there easily.'

It took a lot of pursuasion to get Belinda up on to the ledge and to convince her to crawl forwards under the low roof.

The splash of cascading water was all around them as they edged themselves carefully down into yet another cavern. It was filled with a dark, troubled flood of water, but the light showed a way round. The size of the cavern only emphasised how dim their lamplight was getting.

Holding hands, they edged round the lake, too tired to speak as they helped one another over the rocks.

'Oh, no!' Tracy's voice was filled with despair as the yellow light faded. 'Don't go out on us. Not *now!*'

'We've had it,' said Belinda flatly. The circle of light closed in on them.

'Look!' said Holly. '*Look!*'

Only a few metres away the rocks glowed with a different sort of light. Not the yellow of electric light, but the soft white glow of daylight.

'That's it!' shouted Tracy. 'We've done it. It's the way out.'

Nothing had ever lifted their spirits more than that simple glow of sunlight falling down on to the rocks. They scrambled towards it with renewed strength. It was a long, upwards-pointing fissure, pushing its way up through the dense rock. They panted with laughter as they climbed up those last few feet.

171

Tracy felt earth under her hands. She heaved herself upwards and came tumbling out on to the bright hillside.

'Sunlight!' Holly cried. 'Belinda, we're out!'

The three friends lay in the long grass, feeling the warm sunlight beating down on them.

'I knew we'd find a way,' said Belinda. 'Oh, *warmth*! At last!'

'What do you mean, you knew?' said Tracy. 'You were all for curling up and dying down there.'

'It was all part of my masterplan,' said Belinda. 'I knew if I pretended to give up, it'd spur you two on.'

Holly laughed softly. 'You had me fooled,' she said.

It was a while before they could do any more than lie there basking in the heat.

Holly was the first to sit up and look around. She crawled to the edge of the hill and looked down. Below them the mud-red waters of the Bloody Well poured out of the crack in the hillside.

'We're in *some* kind of mess, guys,' said Tracy. She stared at Belinda. 'You look like you've spent the day in a mud bath.'

'You're not much better,' said Belinda. 'Let's get home, shall we?'

Tracy nodded. 'When I get home I'm going to have the longest shower ever,' she said.

'Do you think the police will have arrived yet?' said Holly. 'Professor Rothwell must have called them ages ago. We ought to tell them about Mallory. I wonder if he managed to find his way out.'

'I hope not,' said Belinda. 'I hope he's still stuck down there. It'd serve him right.'

Holly stood up. 'We've got to find out,' she said. 'Don't forget, he's still got the statue.'

'I want to go home,' wailed Belinda. 'Haven't we done enough today?'

Holly pulled her to her feet. 'I'm not leaving until we know what's happened,' she said. 'The police are probably already up at the cave. Professor Rothwell is bound to have told them where we went. Come on, Belinda, it'll only take us a few minutes to go back and check. Besides, we've got to go back that way to pick up our bikes.'

The three girls made a curious sight as they headed through the trees. Tracy and Holly were covered in dirt and grime, and Belinda was spattered from head to foot with the red mud.

They felt elated after their escape. Linking arms, they talked animatedly about their ordeal, still hardly able to believe that they had come through it unscathed.

There was no sign of the police near the cave mouth. Had the professor not called them after all, wondered Holly.

They came to a sudden halt, their voices fading as they saw the figure half-lying at the entrance to the caves.

It was John Mallory.

His head was thrown back, his arms limp at his sides and his legs stretched out.

'Careful,' said Belinda as they approached him. 'He's dangerous.'

His eyes were closed and his face was locked in a grimace of pain. A livid red weal showed on the side of his face where Belinda had hit him with the dobbie stone. Lying across his open palm was the golden statue.

His eyes opened as he heard them. He lifted his head.

'Help me,' he moaned. 'I think I've broken my ankle.'

'Don't trust him,' said Belinda. 'He fell when he was chasing me, but he might be trying to kid us about how badly he's hurt.'

'I don't think so,' said Tracy, kneeling by his foot. 'It looks really bad.' Above his shoe the swelling of his injury was clearly visible.

'Don't worry,' said Tracy. 'We'll help you.'

Belinda stared down at him. 'You don't deserve to be helped,' she said angrily. 'What help did you give us? You were going to leave us down there.'

Mallory shook his head. 'I'd have sent help,' he said.

Holly picked up the statue. Mallory made a feeble effort to grab it back. He winced and his arm fell.

'We know it was you who stole the things from

Hob's Mound,' said Holly. 'And you're going to admit it, or we'll leave you here.'

'Yes, yes,' murmured Mallory. 'I'll admit anything you like. Just get some help.'

'Could you walk if we supported you?' asked Tracy.

'I . . . I think so,' said Mallory.

Tracy looked round at her friends. 'We could try to get him to the Black Mill,' she said.

They managed to get Mallory to his feet, Holly on one side and Tracy on the other.

Belinda walked behind, still suspicious, her eyes watching for any sudden movement from the limping man. But his injury seemed genuine enough. Even if his ankle wasn't broken, it was certainly a very bad sprain.

It took a long time to get Mallory down through the woods and into the clearing that led to the Black Mill.

There was a police car outside the front of the mill.

'He called them after all,' said Belinda. 'Well done, the professor. I wonder why they didn't go up to the . . .' Her voice faded. Parked alongside the police car was an ambulance.

A young man in the green overalls of a paramedic stood at the back of the ambulance.

'Help!' called Holly.

The man stared at them in astonishment, as if he couldn't quite believe what he was seeing. He ran forward, relieving the exhausted girls of the injured man's weight.

'What's happened to you?' asked the man.

'It's a long story,' said Tracy. 'But what's with the ambulance? Has someone been hurt?'

'It's the old man,' said the paramedic. 'He phoned through for the police, but when they got here he'd collapsed.'

'Oh, no,' said Holly. 'Is he going to be all right?'

'It's not clear,' said the man. 'We'll do all we can.'

The three friends ran forwards. Professor Rothwell lay in the back of the ambulance under a blanket. He seemed to be unconscious.

'Never mind about that old fool,' snarled John Mallory. 'I want to speak to the police.' He glared at Belinda. 'I want that girl charged with assault.'

Belinda stared at him in disbelief.

'These girls are involved in the theft of a priceless golden statue,' said Mallory, his eyes glinting with malice. 'I want them prosecuted for theft and assault!'

The ambulance had gone, speeding Professor Rothwell to hospital. John Mallory sat in the professor's armchair, his swollen ankle supported on a low table. Holly and her friends stood in shocked silence, under the watchful eyes of two police officers.

'I want these girls locked up,' said Mallory. 'Along with that Fairfax woman. They're in this together. I can tell you everything. The whole story.'

'Don't listen to him,' said Tracy. 'He's just going to tell you a pack of lies.'

One of the officers frowned at her. 'You'll get a chance to speak in a minute, miss,' he said. He turned to Mallory. 'What exactly are you saying, sir?'

'I'm telling you that these three girls have been working with Professor Fairfax to steal that statue.' He pointed towards the golden statue in Holly's hand. 'Do you know about the dig at Hob's Mound?'

'We know about it, sir,' said the officer. 'There was a robbery. Professor Fairfax is at the station now, helping us with our enquiries. Now what's all this about the statue?'

'The Fairfax woman told you it had been stolen, didn't she?' said Mallory. 'That was a lie. She hid it. She faked being attacked. She even got these girls to imply that I had something to do with it.' He glared at the girls. 'That's why they were at the police station yesterday, isn't it? To try and implicate me.'

'He's lying,' cried Belinda. 'Professor Fairfax *was* attacked.' She looked at the officers. 'It was Professor Rothwell. He hit Professor Fairfax and took the statue. Ask him!'

177

'I'm afraid it may be some time before Professor Rothwell is able to answer any questions,' said one of the officers.

'You can't believe anything that crazy old man tells you,' said Mallory. 'He's involved as well. They're conspiring together to frame me because I refused to have anything to do with selling the statue. You see,' he continued, 'I knew too much about what was going on. The Fairfax woman asked me to meet her here yesterday. She had the statue with her. She tried to pursuade me to sell it for her. I refused and left. And the next thing I knew the police had picked me up and I was told she had been attacked and robbed.' He pointed a finger towards the girls. 'I came back here to speak to the old man, to try and persuade him to hand the statue over to the authorities. He admitted that it had been hidden up in the caves. I went to get it, but these girls attacked me. Look at me! Look at what they did to me.'

'What we did to *you*?' gasped Belinda. She stared at the officers. 'It's all lies,' she said. 'He chased us into the caves. I was defending myself.'

Mallory gave a grim smile. 'Are you going to believe them rather than me?' he snarled. 'They're friends of the Fairfax woman.'

'There's a small problem with your story, sir,' said one of the officers. 'You see, these girls didn't come to the police station yesterday to talk about you. They came to make a statement about a different matter. A matter concerning this statue. And their statements to us don't tally with your suggestion that they're working with Professor Fairfax.'

John Mallory's eyes narrowed. Holly thought he looked like a snake.

She turned to the officer. 'I've found something else out since we spoke to you,' she said. 'I can prove that Professor Fairfax had nothing to do with stealing the things from Hob's Mound.' She glanced at Mallory's angry, twisted face. 'I can prove it was *him*!'

'Liar!' cried Mallory.

'I'm not a liar,' said Holly. 'Look at his hands. Look at that rash on his hands. It comes from itching powder I spilt on the bags that were stolen.' Holly explained about her accident in the caravan. 'Everyone who's touched those bags has come up in that rash,' she said. She looked at the officers. 'Professor Fairfax doesn't have the rash. She *can't* have touched those bags.'

The police officers turned to Mallory. 'Would you like to comment on this, sir?' asked one of them.

'I'm saying nothing without a solicitor,' snapped Mallory. 'And I demand to have my injuries treated. Injuries inflicted on me by these girls.'

'I think we'd all better go to the station,' said one of the officers. 'A doctor will see to you.' He looked at the girls. 'And I imagine you'll want to

179

clean yourselves up a bit while we send for your parents.'

Holly sat in the interview room at the police station. Mr and Mrs Adams sat on either side of her as a woman inspector took down everything she had to say.

In similar rooms, Tracy and Belinda were going through the same process.

'What will happen to Anne Fairfax?' Holly asked anxiously.

The officer looked down her notes. 'If what you've told us is correct it clears her of having anything to do with the break-in at the dig,' she said. 'But I'm afraid she's going to be in a lot of trouble over the theft of this statue from the museum.'

'You'll arrest her?' asked Holly.

'Professor Fairfax is already here,' said the inspector. 'She's being questioned about her confessions. Although from what you've just told us, we're going to have to look into some of the statements she's made a lot more carefully.'

'And Chris Lambert?' asked Holly.

'There's a car waiting at his lodgings,' said the police inspector. 'He'll be picked up as soon as he returns. We'll want to question him, although from what Professor Fairfax has told us, he's in the clear.'

'Can Holly go now?' asked Mr Adams. 'She's told you everything she knows.'

The inspector smiled. 'We shan't be needing Holly or her friends any more at the moment.' She stood up, looking at the state of Holly's clothes. 'I think you'd probably like a bath, eh?'

Holly nodded.

They were shown out to the reception area.

'Can we wait and see how Tracy and Belinda have got on?' Holly asked her parents.

'I think we probably should,' said Mrs Adams. She shook her head. 'What are we going to do with you, Holly? Look at the state you're in.'

Holly sighed and sank into a chair. 'It was terrible in those caves,' she said. 'I really thought we might not get out.'

Mrs Adams put her arm round Holly's shoulders. 'It's all over now, love,' she said. 'You'll be home safe and sound soon.'

They heard footsteps in the corridor. Mrs Hayes and Mrs Foster came towards them with Belinda and Tracy at their sides.

'I am never going to understand how you three girls get yourselves mixed up in these things,' said Mrs Hayes.

Belinda smiled tiredly. 'You and me, both,' she said.

'At least everyone's safe and sound,' said Mrs Foster. 'That's what matters in the end.'

Holly's parents stood up. 'Home?' said Mr Adams.

'Home!' sighed Holly.

They looked round at a sudden disturbance from the entrance to the police station.

Holly's eyes widened. Chris Lambert, his face a mask of shock, was being escorted into the police station by two officers.

He stared at Holly.

He started towards her. 'What have you told them?' he cried. 'What have you been saying about Anne?'

'I had to tell them,' said Holly, looking in anguish at the frightened young man. 'That whole business with the statue was a fraud!'

'I *know* that!' he shouted. 'I know all about it. But you've got it wrong! You've got it completely wrong! It was nothing to do with Anne. She didn't have anything to do with it.' He struggled in the restraining grip of the policemen.

'It was *me*!' he shouted. 'It was all me!'

13 Confessions

'Christopher! Don't say anything!' Holly's head snapped round at the sound of this new voice. At the far end of the corridor Anne Fairfax stood at an open door, a policeman at her side.

'But they think you stole the statue,' shouted Chris. 'I've got to tell them the truth.'

The inspector who had been interviewing Holly appeared from the side room.

'What's all this noise?' she said. She looked at Chris. 'You're the Lambert boy?'

'Yes. It's me you want. Anne had nothing to do with taking the statue,' said Chris. 'I don't know what you've been told, but Anne had nothing to do with it. She didn't know anything about it.'

'Christopher!' said Anne Fairfax. 'Don't! I've already confessed to them. About the statue and about the robbery at the dig.'

Chris stared at her. 'Why did you do that?' he said. He looked at the inspector. 'She's just trying to protect me. Let her go. I'll tell you everything.'

The inspector frowned at him. 'I think you'd

better,' she said. 'I think it's time we were told the truth.'

Anne Fairfax ran down the corridor. The girls and their parents stepped aside in surprise as she caught hold of Chris's hand.

'Why did you do it?' she implored, staring into his eyes. 'Why couldn't you have just waited? We'd have found everything we hoped for once the barrow had been opened.'

'I was afraid there'd be nothing in there,' said Chris. 'I didn't want to risk that. I knew how much you needed to find something important. I did it for you. For us. So we could go to France together.'

'Oh, Christopher!' said Anne Fairfax. 'It wasn't *that* important. Not so important that you should have stolen those things from the caravan as well. Did you think I wouldn't guess it was you?'

Chris stared at her. 'I didn't,' he said. 'I buried the statue, but I had nothing to do with the robbery.'

Anne Fairfax's mouth fell open. 'But I thought you took those things. That's why I confessed to it. Once I realised the truth about the statue, I just assumed you'd taken the other things to get me the money.'

'I think you'd both better come with me,' said the inspector, looking from Anne Fairfax to Chris. 'I think there's a good deal you'll be wanting to tell me now, isn't there?'

The inspector nodded towards the interview room.

'In there, please. Both of you,' she said.

Holly stared in amazement as Chris and Anne Fairfax were led, hand in hand, into the interview room and the door was closed behind them.

'So it *was* Chris who switched the statues,' breathed Belinda. 'Professor Fairfax was just covering for him.'

'I wish someone would explain all this to *me*,' said Mrs Hayes. She looked at the other parents. 'Do *you* have any idea what all this is about?'

'Chris and Professor Fairfax were seeing each other secretly,' said Holly. 'That's why Professor Fairfax made those confessions. To *protect* him.' She looked at her parents. 'Can we stay to find out what will happen?'

'No,' said Mrs Adams firmly. 'It's time you were going home, Holly. I'm sure the police will let you know everything in good time.'

'And I would like to know exactly how you girls got yourself involved in all this,' said Mrs Hayes.

Belinda looked awkwardly at her. 'It's a long story,' she said.

Mrs Foster sighed. '*Another* long story,' she said. She smiled disbelievingly at the other parents, her arm round Tracy's shoulders. 'I think I'll get you home before you start on your explanation, Tracy. I'm not sure I'll be able to cope with it standing up.'

185

The three girls were taken out to the waiting cars.

It seemed that the final revelation in the story of the golden statue was going to have to wait.

Holly was too tired to do anything other than take a bath and climb wearily into bed when she got home.

A little later, Mrs Adams brought her up a cup of hot chocolate. She sat on the edge of the bed.

'What with you and Jamie,' she sighed, 'there's never a dull moment around here.'

'What's Jamie been up to?' asked Holly, sitting up in bed and sipping from the mug of chocolate.

'Didn't you see the state he left the garden in?'

'Oh, that,' said Holly. 'I wondered when you'd notice.'

'We noticed, OK,' said Mrs Adams. 'Your father has made him fill all the holes in. He's lucky he's not been grounded for the rest of the month.' She smiled. 'I hope all your adventures have given you enough information to finish writing that article of yours.'

'The article!' exclaimed Holly. 'I'd nearly forgotten. It's got to be handed in on Tuesday at the latest.' She looked for her notebook. She'd left it on her bedside table, but it didn't seem to be there any more. She made as if to scramble out of bed.

'No!' said Mrs Adams. 'You're not doing any

writing now. It can wait until tomorrow. I want you to go to sleep.'

Holly sank back into the pillows.

'OK,' she said wearily. 'But I won't be able to sleep, I've got far too much to think about.'

Mrs Adams stood up. 'Sleep,' she said. 'Think about it in the morning.' She switched the light off and left the room.

Despite what she had said, Holly fell asleep almost immediately. The exertions of the day had exhausted her, and even the puzzle of the missing notebook couldn't keep her awake.

'Holly Adams?'

Holly looked up. It was the first lesson of the day. She had spoken briefly to Tracy and Belinda before school began, but they hadn't had time for a proper discussion. That would have to wait until later.

The school secretary stood at the classroom door.

'Miss Horswell would like to see you in her office immediately,' said the secretary.

Surprised at being called out of class like this, Holly followed the secretary to the head-teacher's office.

Belinda and Tracy were already there. Miss Horswell sat at her desk. At her side stood the woman police inspector who had interviewed Holly the previous day.

'The inspector tells me you three girls have been

very helpful in solving a crime,' said Miss Horswell. She smiled. 'She asked to have a word with you.'

The inspector nodded. 'I thought you deserved to be amongst the first to hear,' she said. 'Professor Fairfax has been cleared of all charges relating to the theft of the statue from the museum. Christopher Lambert has given us a full confession.'

'I knew he did it all along,' said Belinda. 'We worked it all out ages ago.'

'Professor Fairfax made her confessions to protect him,' said the inspector. 'Their friendship has been a lot closer than anyone knew for some months now. Christopher Lambert came up with the plan to bury the statue while he was working on the Celtic finds in the museum. He had the opportunity to make a fair copy of the real thing out of the clay used in the shop where he was lodging. But he knew a copy wouldn't stand up to the sort of scrutiny the university would give it. Which is why he put the copy in the museum and buried the real statue at Hob's Mound.'

'And Professor Fairfax had no idea he was planning all this?' said Holly.

'Evidently not,' said the inspector. 'She became suspicious later, when the statue was taken to the university for authentication. She realised it was *too* similar to the one that had been found at Elfbolt Hill. From what she has told me, it seems that there were markings on the statue that were exactly the same as those on the Elfbolt Hill statue. Which is why she decided to take the statue to the man who had originally discovered it.'

'Professor Rothwell!' cried Belinda.

'Exactly,' said the inspector. 'She hoped that she would be able to find out the truth from him. If her suspicions were correct, she realised that it had to have been Christopher Lambert who had done the switch. No one else would take that sort of risk for her. She hoped to be able to cover the whole thing up before he got into trouble. But it seems that Professor Rothwell was too confused to tell her anything, so she left him without her suspicions being confirmed.'

'And then Professor Rothwell hit her and took the statue before she could do anything else,' said Tracy. 'But do you know exactly what happened over at the mill? Do you know what John Mallory was up to?'

'I think so,' said the inspector. 'Mallory's part in this goes back to the fact that he wanted Professor Fairfax taken off the dig. He knew she wouldn't let him have any of the things she found, so he set about trying to discredit her. He broke into the caravan and stole the things in there, intending to plant them on Professor Fairfax and then to call the police anonymously and suggest they search her car. He followed her to the mill, hoping for an opportunity to plant the stolen items on her.'

'That's right,' said Belinda. 'I heard him say something like that in the mill. He must have

189

followed her there and put the stuff in her car while she was talking to Professor Rothwell.'

The inspector nodded. 'He's admitted doing that,' she said. She smiled at Holly. 'He could hardly deny it, after the evidence you gave us about the rash on his hands. But when we picked him up originally, we were looking for the stolen statue. He didn't have it on him, and there was no real evidence to suggest he was involved, so we had to let him go.'

'And he must have guessed afterwards that Professor Rothwell had taken the statue,' said Holly.

'Mallory knew how valuable the statue was,' said the inspector. 'He knew he'd be able to sell it and disappear with the proceeds if only he could lay his hands on it. And he might have got away with it, if you girls hadn't been there.'

'We sure showed him, didn't we?' said Tracy.

'You did,' agreed the inspector. 'Although you'd have been wiser to have contacted us rather than put yourselves in so much danger.'

Belinda gave her a grin. 'We didn't *know* we'd end up lost in those caves,' she said. 'We only wanted to make sure Mallory didn't get away with the statue. We knew Professor Rothwell was going to phone you.' A worried frown came over her face. 'How is Professor Rothwell?'

'He's in hospital,' said the inspector. 'He's suffering from nervous exhaustion. They're hopeful he'll make a full recovery, but he'll be needing a lot of medical help before he's fully fit. Professor Fairfax has refused to press charges for his attack on her, so it's not likely we'll be needing to speak to him for the time being.'

'And the statue?' asked Holly.

'We're keeping it as evidence for the moment,' said the inspector. 'But it will eventually be going back to the museum.'

'So that's it?' said Tracy. 'Everything's been solved, thanks to us.'

The inspector nodded. 'Thanks very largely to you three, yes,' she said. 'And your evidence will see to it that John Mallory is brought to justice.'

'Is Chris in a lot of trouble?' asked Holly.

'It looks that way,' said the inspector. 'But I'm sure Professor Fairfax's evidence about his motives will be taken into account when he comes to trial.'

'Well,' said Miss Horswell. 'It looks like you girls have been very helpful.' She smiled, standing up. 'I don't think we need keep you from your lessons any longer.' She showed the Mystery Club and the inspector to the door.

'I imagine you'll be writing about this for the school magazine, Holly?' said Miss Horswell as the inspector left.

'I've already started,' said Holly. 'I've just got time to finish the article before Steffie Smith's deadline.'

The three friends headed for their classrooms,

Holly already piecing her article together in her head.

Willow Dale schoolgirls solve the crime of the fake statue. The Mystery Club does it again!

That evening the three girls met together in Holly's bedroom to finish the article. But there was a problem. Holly still couldn't find the Mystery Club's red notebook.

'You know,' said Belinda, as she and Tracy helped Holly search. 'There's still something a bit odd about the things Professor Rothwell said to me.'

'What kind of odd?' asked Tracy.

'Well, he went on about how the dobbie stone would protect me, didn't he?' said Belinda. 'And it *did*. If I hadn't bashed Mallory with it when he had me cornered in the caves, I dread to think what he might have done to me. And he said I would be drawn down into the darkness. And I was.' She looked at her friends with an uneasy grin. 'It's a bit strange, don't you think?'

'I'd rather *not* think about it, if you don't mind,' said Tracy. 'If I start thinking about things like that I'm likely to end up as flaky as the Mad Professor.'

'You're right,' said Holly. 'It *is* odd, but we've got more important things to think about right now. Like where is that blessed notebook?' She hunted under her bed. 'It was on my bedside table yesterday, I'm sure it was,' she said. 'Someone must have moved it.'

'It must be around somewhere,' said Belinda. 'Who'd bother taking it?'

'Jamie!' said Holly. 'He said he was going to get his revenge on us. I bet it was him.'

'OK,' said Tracy. 'Let's get him!'

They took Jamie completely by surprise, piling into his room and pinning him to the floor before he could escape.

'What have you done with our notebook, you pest?' shouted Holly, sitting on him. 'I know it was you.'

Jamie squirmed under them. 'I'll tell you, I'll tell you!' he yelled. 'I buried it in the garden. Get off me and I'll show you where.'

'You buried it?' exclaimed Holly. 'I'm really going to kill you for this.'

'I'll dig it up again,' gasped Jamie. 'It was only a *joke*!'

They let him up.

'It had better not be ruined,' said Holly.

'It's in a plastic bag,' said Jamie. 'Anyway, you deserved it, after trying to make me look stupid with those coins.'

The three girls frog-marched Jamie down the stairs and out into the garden.

Tracy ran to get a spade and Holly pushed it into his hands.

'Dig!' she said. 'And if there's a single mark on it, you're going to wish you had never been born.'

'It'll be OK,' said Jamie, thrusting the spade into the soft earth. 'I don't know why you're making such a fuss about it.'

'You'll find out if it's ruined,' warned Holly.

It only took the removal of a couple of spades full of earth before the plastic bag containing the Mystery Club's red notebook was revealed. Jamie bent down and picked it up.

'See?' he said. 'It's perfectly OK.'

Holly took it from him and pulled the notebook out of the muddy bag.

'Well?' said Jamie. 'What did I tell you?'

The notebook seemed undamaged. Holly turned on Jamie with a fierce grin.

'Let's see how well you survive a few hours under the earth,' she said. She looked at her friends. 'Come on, you two,' she said. 'What say we bury him up to his neck and leave him for the ants to get!'

With a shriek, Jamie ducked away from the three girls and ran towards the house.

'After him!' shouted Holly. 'Don't let him get away!'

They were just running up the stairs in pursuit of the fleeing Jamie when there was a ring at the doorbell.

Holly went to answer it.

Kurt was standing there. Behind him she could see his father's car.

'What's going on?' he asked, seeing Tracy and Belinda on the stairs behind her.

'Jamie thinks it's funny to bury our notebook in the garden,' said Holly. 'So we're going to see how funny he finds it when we bury *him*!'

Kurt laughed. 'You can if you like,' he said. 'But I think you might prefer to come with me and my dad. We've just heard – Professor Fairfax has finally broken into the burial chamber at Hob's Mound. Apparently there's loads of brilliant stuff in there. Don't you want to come and see?'

All thoughts of revenge on Jamie were forgotten as the three girls packed themselves into the back of Mr Welford's car and he drove them off to the dig.

'I hope it's the real thing this time,' said Tracy.

'Oh, yes,' said Mr Welford. 'It's the real thing, OK. It's a treasure trove in there, from what I've been told. Oh,' he added. 'Holly? Kurt tells me you solved most of this mystery. How would you fancy writing it up for the *Express*?'

'I'd love to!' exclaimed Holly. 'Can I? An article of my own in the *Express*?'

'Just hold it a minute here,' said Belinda. 'There were three of us involved in this mystery. I don't see why Holly should get to write the article.'

'I'm the best writer,' said Holly. 'That's why.'

'You've got the biggest head, you mean,' said

Tracy. 'If there's going to be a piece in the *Express* I reckon we should *all* have a hand in it.'

'That's right,' said Belinda. 'For once I agree with Tracy.'

'OK, OK,' cried Mr Welford. 'Anything you say. You can *all* write it, between you.'

Belinda grinned. 'That's exactly how it should be,' she said. 'And we can put in the bit about me losing my favourite sweat-shirt in the process.'

'You're kidding?' said Tracy, looking at Belinda's replacement sweat-shirt. 'The one you're wearing now is exactly the same! The same green and everything.'

'OK,' said Belinda. 'We can write about how I sacrificed *one* of my favourite sweat-shirts. I don't mind. So long as I get star billing.'

Tracy and Holly jumped on Belinda and she let out a stifled yell of laughter as the car sped towards the treasure at Hob's Mound.

DEADLY GAMES

by Fiona Kelly

Holly, Belinda and Tracy are back in the
ninth thrilling adventure in the
Mystery Club series, published by
Knight Books.

Here is the first chapter . . .

1 A big break

Steffie Smith really was a pain! These days, she never printed an article in *Winformation* without messing it up completely! Holly scrunched up the latest copy of the school magazine and marched down the corridor.

'Uh-oh!' Tracy said, peering out of her classroom. 'Holly looks real mad about something!' Holly ignored her. She headed for the library and the *Winformation* desk there.

Tracy beckoned Belinda and they both set off in hot pursuit.

'Shh!' Belinda warned, looking over Tracy's shoulder. 'I think it's something to do with the magazine!' she said.

They followed more cautiously now.

Holly was in no mood for fooling around. In fact, she'd hardly ever felt this cross about anything in her entire life. She swung open the library door and turned into the corner partitioned off for school magazine business. Sure enough, Steffie was there.

'Look at this!' Holly slammed her copy of

Winformation down on Steffie's desk. It was open at the sports pages. She didn't even pause for breath. 'OK, so lately you've given me all the sports reporting! I've gone to all the first year soccer matches. I faithfully reported every deadly dull rounders ball ever thrown! I wrote virtually the entire sports pages single-handed. And what do you do? You miss out the scores! Holly felt her face grow hot with anger.

Steffie glanced up. 'Have I? Oh, yes.' She looked down again at the piece she was working on, half-written in front of her.

'Is that all?' Holly stepped back amazed. She'd expected excuses, maybe even an apology.

'What? Oh, sorry,' Steffie said. 'Listen, I have to get on with this review. What's the name of Juliet's family in *Romeo and Juliet*, can you remember?'

Holly couldn't believe her ears. 'Capulet,' she said.

'Thanks,' Steffie said absent-mindedly. She jotted it down. 'Who played Romeo in the school production?'

By this time Holly was wide-eyed, but her brain was racing. 'Tom Benson. Uh, Steffie, you look as if you're under a bit of pressure here.' She leaned both hands on the edge of Steffie's cluttered desk. Holly's natural desire to help out someone in trouble was winning through. Anyway, she caught scent of an interesting problem behind Steffie's odd behaviour. 'Do you need any help?' she asked.

'Maybe,' Steffie sighed.

'Well,' Holly said, trying to keep her voice calm, 'why don't you let me finish off that review?' What she really meant was, 'I'd kill to do the arts pages.' Until now, Steffie had hogged them all. Holly braced herself for the usual bossy Steffie Smith knockback.

'OK,' Steffie said quietly. She handed over the scrappy paper with its few scrawls. 'Two hundred and fifty words for Wednesday, please.'

Holly grabbed it. 'Thanks!' She thought at top speed and decided she would push her luck just a little bit further. 'And I was wondering about something else . . .'

'Yes?' Steffie had turned to the empty computer screen and was staring blankly at it.

'Well, would you let me have a go at a couple of mystery pages for the next issue?

'Mystery pages?' Steffie frowned. Then she shrugged. 'Yeah, why not? Go ahead, do what you want.' And she turned back to the empty screen.

She could not believe her luck – what on earth was wrong with Steffie?

'What's wrong with Steffie?' Tracy asked.

They were eating lunch in the dining-hall.

'Who knows.' Holly wasn't interested right then. 'All I know is that she's given me a double spread for mystery news in the next issue! Isn't that great?'

'That's quite a mystery in itself,' Belinda quipped. 'Why on earth would Steffie want to give up part of her precious magazine?'

'Well, she did! And she gave me the *Romeo and Juliet* review!' Holly insisted.

Belinda gave a slow smile. 'Well done, Holly. You've been wanting a chance like that for ages.'

Holly nodded. 'I know!'

'Wow, there must be something really wrong!' Tracy said. 'I can't think what could make a girl like Steffie look so down. Maybe it's boyfriend trouble.' She shrugged and went over to talk to Miss Baron, the music teacher.

Holly began to scribble notes for the *Romeo and Juliet* review. Suddenly Belinda broke in with, 'No, it doesn't look like boyfriend trouble to me.'

'What?' Holly broke off. 'Oh, you're still going on about Steffie? Listen, as long as she doesn't change her mind about the mystery pages, I'm happy!'

But Belinda kept up the jokey investigation of Steffie's problems. 'From what I hear, Steffie's given up boyfriends to concentrate on her career. She eats, sleeps and lives for *Winformation*. That's what's so peculiar about her handing everything over to you.'

'Thanks a lot!' Holly stood up, pretending to be offended. 'I really appreciate that vote of confidence!' The bell had gone for afternoon registration and Holly started packing her bag.

'No, I didn't mean that, Holly. I'm just saying

how dedicated she is. It's not boyfriend trouble with Steffie. I'd say it was family problems!'

Holly glanced at Belinda. 'Family problems?' she repeated.

'Yeah, they make you awfully moody.' Belinda insisted. 'Moody and unpredictable, like Steffie is now. I'm telling you, that girl definitely has family problems!'

The three girls met up after school as usual.

'Well, since we've no actual mystery on our hands at the moment, what do you two say to going into town for an ice-cream?' Tracy suggested. 'In the park, the ice-cream parlour, or the van in the carpark?'

'The carpark!' Belinda cried. 'It's nearest, and I'm starving!'

Holly and Tracy laughed. Belinda was *always* starving.

'I can't stop long,' Holly told them as they perched, ice-creams in hand, on a low wall by the flower-beds. 'I've got to work fast on Wednesday's deadlines!'

'Hey!' Tracy said softly. 'Don't look now, but here comes your beloved editor. I wonder what she's up to?'

They looked over to where Tracy was pointing. Across the carpark by an expensive little boutique, they spotted Steffie Smith herself. She still looked miserable. They watched as she checked up and down the street and looked anxiously at her watch. Then, up drove the shiniest, smoothest looking sports car Holly had ever seen. It was a red convertible. The driver pulled up beside Steffie and stepped out.

'Can this be real?' Tracy gasped.

The driver looked as if he'd stepped out of a Hollywood movie. He was about twenty years old, with a fabulous haircut. He was tall and handsome. His clothes were casual, but clearly expensive.

Steffie greeted him with a tiny peck on the cheek. He put one arm round her shoulder. She turned her face away and stood clear of him. He leant against the car, apparently trying to explain something to her. Steffie shook her head. She spread her palms, arguing, telling him something he didn't want to hear. He put his hands in his pockets, looking stubborn. He shook his head back at her.

'They're having a row!' Belinda breathed.

'Why would anyone row with someone that good looking?' Tracy said.

'Shh!' Holly warned. If there were any clues, they didn't want to miss them.

Steffie had stopped arguing. She hung her head, and the two of them stood in silence, unaware of the envious stares of passers-by at the dream car. Then Steffie began again, talking at him, tugging at his sleeve. *No*, he was saying; *no!* Steffie turned away, said one last thing over her shoulder before she walked off.

Tracy and Holly stared after the disappearing figure.

Belinda looked thoughfully at the young man as he climbed back into his car. He revved the engine and slid off towards the main road in the opposite direction to Steffie. He didn't pause, and he didn't look back.

'See, what did I say? Boyfriend trouble!' Tracy declared triumphantly. 'Anyhow, I don't think it's anything the Mystery Club can get involved in.' She shrugged. 'Just a little argument, I guess.' She ate the last bit of her ice-cream and sighed. 'Who ever heard of a Mystery Club minus a mystery?'

'Yes, no need to write this down in the Mystery Club notebook!' Belinda sighed, then gave a little grin.

'I'm not to sure!' Holly said slowly. Was this just a simple boyfriend-girlfriend row?

Belinda watched the red car disappear. 'Poor thing,' she said. She hated it when people argued.

'Who, Steffie?' Holly grabbed her schoolbag, ready to leave. For some reason she disagreed. Normally she would have a soft spot for anyone in trouble, but she couldn't exactly bring herself to feel sorry for Steffie Smith!